N Dy 20.4

THIS GENTLE COMPANION

The hero of this remarkable story is a novelist married to a psychiatric worker, Emilia. Poverty compels him to write a pornographic book, but in doing so he becomes fascinated by the technical problems involved and begins to feel that through this novel he 'grasps a shred of the truth for the first time'. He is obsessed by death (who is 'This Gentle Companion', referred to throughout as She or Her), with whom he has several brushes — an episode in a glider, a neighbour's heart attack, a meeting with a grave digger, a car accident to Emilia herself. This spiritual unease is finally traced back to his sexual obsession in the past with Miriam, whose suicide has planted in him a deep sense of guilt. The impending death of his own mother provides the last impulse towards his reconciliation with our fate.

THIS
GENTLE
COMPANION

by

CARLO
CASTELLANETA

1971
CHATTO & WINDUS
LONDON

Published by
Chatto & Windus Ltd
40 William IV Street
London W.C.2

*

Clarke, Irwin & Co. Ltd
Toronto

ISBN 0 7011 1796 6

Translated from LA DOLCE COMPAGNA

by Sebastian Roberts

Printed in Great Britain
by Ebenezer Baylis & Son Ltd
The Trinity Press, Worcester, and London

CONTENTS

Part One   PAGE   7

Part Two   PAGE   93

Part One

FAR more solid is the stone we come back and stand before, expecting an answer. More solid and inviolable. Few spaces, little margin between, the mark of craftsmanship in the working of the slabs.

I still knew nothing about Her except for a few chance signs I had picked up as I went, and these were hardening at last into a visible question. Even my own image took on a classic air. Calm I must have looked as I stepped along the Ring Road, amid the leaves fallen from the limes that hang down over the old Spanish walls, my steps brushing and no more the cracks in the tar, and it is at this point that the anxiety is soothed into irony — something akin to that of the old masters who painted Judas with the features of an impatient duke or overbearing pope.

The first time, it had happened as I was driving on one of my usual little runs, skirting the Market, with the gates of the Shambles on the other side, the tall chimney-stack, the street was filled with blinding sunlight, and as I shot down into the tunnel (just as a lorry was clanking its way over the iron bridge), the premonition of the end flashed through me like an arrow.

'Did you notice if there was any mail?'

Emilia showed me the letter she held under the parcel, a French stamp, handwriting I knew for Edo's. But nothing registered and no cheque. On the table-cloth a few things only: the wine bottle in the fitting space between us, the packet from which the bread-sticks pointed, the radio talking on unheeded, a hurried kiss that Nixon cannot hear, and I wanted to say to her, it must be films that have turned every familiar gesture into something unbearable, but Emilia was already going, her smile from the doorway so perfect that with a background of Mozart it was nothing less than incredible.

'Are you going to be late?'

'I'll phone you,' she called back as she made for the lift.

The sound of the voice lingers more shattering than any other memory: the inflection, an accent like no other. This is what we should accustom ourselves to: to the thought of leaving behind, we too, something unique, the never-to-be-repeated. Instead, as I waited for the lights to change, I went over a list of practical memoranda in my head (learn to ignore little claims on your time, purchase a microscope, work harder at English) in the certainty that I would never do one of these things.

This is the hour of day I love best: sky and street of one colour, it could be October, the hand moving to the gear-lever unbidden, the roaring of a big jet before it takes off, the mind almost unaware of the body and its muscles, and although the avenue was thronged with cars, there was, first of all, this terrace, perhaps two terraces or more, filled in with tables laid for dinner, the white rectangles of the cloths standing out minute at first, then larger, until they are life-size, now I remembered every detail of the dream, I could make out the carnations in the long, slender vases, we had come a long way to get there, and the three of us were grouped around the table, impelled, God knows why, by the risk of being discovered, even if it was not possible for them to see us from the terraces below, or perhaps just for this reason; so that they could visualize how my hands moved and writhed under the dresses of the two; and we were only at the beginning.

Keep calm, I told them, otherwise they'll notice, but I knew how useless it was, when both of the women were set on accomplishing the thing they had in mind: to make me perform the most unspeakable of acts, perhaps Emilia could explain this to me, the movement a little slow but gay, 'con brio', now I was sure of it, I recognized the metal railing of the air terminal, but not the exact point, because the lens took in nothing but their two bodies, from knees to breasts, bodies without heads amid the jingle of cutlery and glass, of this much I was certain, this moment is always repeated: it was strange that no one observed us, the others stiff at their tables, laughing soundlessly, then there was a jump of a few stills, I can't understand it because Miriam always warns me first: she puts her lips to my ear and murmurs: just see how good at it I am, and she makes the remark sound as casual as can be, but the candle-lights waved to and fro behind the little screens, upon the tables, the terrace railing painted a white which shone phosphorescent in the dark, so that I began to be uneasy about their legs, too, bared all the way to the groin, about that white band of skin they showed off so shamelessly: and lastly I was uneasy about my own self, held to that nightmare by a spectre which conscience had buried a good while before.

We should use stricter judgement, in our dreams.

Paltry images alternate with flashes of revelation. And then the jarring of the door which Emilia closes behind her every morning.

And finally the ringing of the phone.

I stretched out an arm to the bedside table: alarm call, she announced, shake yourself, it's ten o'clock. But I've been awake a good while, and, you know something, I've had a strange dream. Tell me, she says. I can't, not over the phone, I had to explain.

I called her back, at the Centre, after I had taken my shower: a few minutes' wait and then her step sounding in the ear-piece. Nothing, I said to her, I want to write a book about the pain of this world on an ordinary day like today, I'm only afraid that I'm not equal to it.

She must have been on the point of saying it out to me: do you think it's easy to live with you? I hesitated now before I answered her remarks, but only to hit on the exact answer. There was a metallic rattle at one point in our conversation, as if a door had been shut roughly.

'Well, we can discuss it,' said Emilia. 'We've just got a new female patient in, a bad case, I'll tell you later.'

By this time I am ready to go out, I walk in the poorer district, conscious of my privilege of being the only one who can stroll here at this so late hour of the morning, the world becomes a show, faces of the pedestrians, the people shut up in factories, behind the windows of offices, as I myself was for twenty years, a phrase caught in passing, gestures, the faces in the cars, everything that is routine raised up to the exception, a doorway, two legs of a girl which venture in, the cries in the courtyards, and I can guess the first interpretation Emilia would give of my dream material, going by the theory that a dream is the projection of hidden desires.

I had reached the large square that has a record shop on one corner. Look, I went on: two girls on the terrace, the table was laid, and one of the two was Miriam, my hand under the tablecloth felt one and then the other of them, it was all quite natural, but the waiters were watching us, believe me, it was torture, and I stared at the record shop window without distinguishing among the massed sleeves.

'Yes, that's it,' I explain to the girl-assistant. 'Country sounds, but with no musical background, like hen noises, or cicadas . . .'

She did not even look, she replied that no such record exists, and even if it does exist, we do not handle it, she seems quite offended, but look, miss, I should explain everything to her: what this panting after childhood is (and all of us have known it), the inner echo of some few sounds, from a country way of life that you no longer find even in the country, that hen gurgle shaking the afternoon silence and silence rises up clear as white of egg and brings with it images of quiet, the tranquillity that will let me dissolve the scurf of a bad dream, a need for purity, ridiculous word, but without which it is impossible to think of a book on the pain of this world, so I thought: if there was a record of that kind.

'I'm sorry but there isn't. I could make enquiries.'

It was clear that I was going along where chance led me. So now it was too late to keep my appointment, for the discussion with Doctor Y. Or rather I trusted the post to deliver, before noon, some unexpected, liberating missive.

I turned back, and it hurt me not to have been able

to explain my seemingly absurd request to the shop-assistant. But Emilia always says we must make up our minds to it, we can communicate with only two or three other people at most, and after all I communicate with Emilia, with Mozart, and then there are some brief transmissions over the short wave which never come through clear but are full of crackling.

I said to her: I'm afraid of one thing only. I was crossing the avenue in front of our house, without heeding the traffic.

To spend my last days, Emilia, on a bed in a ward.

And yet living with the thought of Her should strengthen us, make us braver, because, by comparison, nothing else that can happen seems terrifying. But I was just beginning to see this, it was no more than a possibility, meanwhile I parked my car and pressed the button in the lift, and, last of all, gave my name to his secretary.

I knew only that I was going to dirty my hands. The question was how badly.

Doctor Y made it clear to me as soon as I had sat myself opposite him in the black-leather arm-chair.

'That novel you published three years ago . . .'

I pointed out that it was five.

'Alright: five years ago. Well, my view is this: a story like that suits us down to the ground, but—no censoring the text—five hundred thousand in advance, the same again when you hand over the typescript. All the situations described in real detail, you've got to call things by their names, you writers are always trying to get poetry into it. None of that. If it's arse, write arse. Clear? We'll add the photographs. All the girls'll be the best Danish models. Could do a de luxe edition. Numbered. We'll see.'

And my good name? Y explains to me — handkerchief polishing spectacle lenses — that I can use a nom-de-plume, that legally I would be completely covered; they do these editions in three languages, distribute them more or less clandestinely, the worst that can happen is confiscation; the author gets two or two and a half million for sure, not to mention foreign rights.

The only demur I had to make was that perhaps it would be better to write a completely new story, seeing that readers would perhaps recognize the thing as mine from the version I had already put out with a respectable publisher.

'Listen, that story of how a woman was corrupted, it really impressed me. Exactly what we want. A great idea. And think of it like this — you won't have all the trouble of dreaming up a new plot. And don't forget. It's got to be at least a hundred and fifty pages long.'

Odd it is how a man will inevitably nourish the illusion that his time is to be long (and in fact burying acquaintances is one of our greatest satisfactions), when the thought of a sudden end should be with us always to make us more wary. I attempted one last evasion: the law that punishes indecency; what limits does that impose exactly.

'No limit at all,' Doctor Y declared.

'No thanks,' I refused the cigarette.

'Here. Copy of the contract. A secret document, of course. Everything there, but the title of our book. Five hundred thousand when you sign. Manuscript to be handed over inside three months. And — keep that character, the married woman, will you.'

Man is, of necessity, vile.

'Where do I sign?' I heard myself asking.

If this were all, it would not be so bad: to lose yourself in the mists of sleep, sink down into the quiet beating of your own body, the arteries running fresh, breathing rhythmic, a well-regulated system of diastole and systole, and the sounds of another world that goes on distinct from us.

Emilia reproaches me for sleeping more than I need. I dare not tell her that I consider it the surest way of prolonging youth, the state of grace when everything is still in play, open to a thousand chances; because the hardest thing to accept is our averageness, our failure to reach, even in the evil we do, any greatness: caution and long-suffering hailed as virtues; prodigality and grim determination branded as vices. But what we are to do with it all under a ton of earth, the sages do not say.

Better to try the news, the paper waits on the door-step as it does every morning, and by the streak of light from the strip-blind you can run your eye over the headlines. And the stars say that money will unexpectedly come your way this week, improving your finances considerably. Changes for the better in the future, too, which looks cloudless; not one worry in your sky.

It is a kind of abasing yourself when you give in and read, or listen to, what you loathe, perhaps because a shadow of doubt works its way into your well-founded contempt, especially if the radio, switched on this moment, says, hug me, I want to cry.

How much time has passed? The newspaper lay on my chest, the voice sang, just to cry with you, the objects in the room began to stand out clear in the light; a limp hand recalling childhood, I could see Emilia entering her office, hanging up her coat, opening her desk diary, having left here on this sheet her body's warmth and me sunk in the most delightful sloth.

The shower chased every thought away. My mother taught me never to go out without a handkerchief, and always to be clean just in case they have to rush me to the first aid station. So I slipped a quarto sheet into my portable, tapped 'Part One', and then went out to see mother herself.

I took the bus to the centre of town, got down at the tube station, and there, at the bookstall, I found that my short story had come out in one of the magazines she is in the habit of reading.

'I saw it alright,' she says, 'but I haven't read it yet. Yes, I saw it, but last night my eyes were hurting.'

At that moment what I was watching in her were those two lines that curve from nose to mouth, and the slack underlip, hanging down, like a first sign of what would soon happen to her: shrunken, the wrists, a network of faint scales, hollowed-out cheeks, the bones above them protruding.

'If that pension was to come through for me, even you wouldn't bother to look me up like this, once a month, it's only to bring the money.'

'Now, what in the name . . .'

I tried to give her heart, knowing only too well that no one could, at that moment or any other, and least of all when she has turned side on, to light the gas and set the percolator over the ring, and I can see the sinews in her neck quivering like strings as she curses quietly to herself, and shakes the match out.

'Luckily there's Signora Bernotti on this floor, she's always brought me hot soup. If she gave up, I could easily drop dead.'

Her fever bout has whittled away what fleshiness was left at her throat and her larynx comes and goes in a grotesque jig, appalling to watch, like this dressing-gown she has worn for twenty years, or the grease-lacquered handle to the window, and she talks on, grudgingly.

'And suppose I were to drop dead, it would be all for the better.'

I wanted to tell her that Doctor Berry has found the astronauts in perfect shape although they have been in orbit for sixty-four hours now, but she went on.

'Anyway, even Signora Bernotti has no life to speak of, since that son of hers died, who always stayed with her.'

'What son? I don't remember.'

Same old story: I never remember anything, my head screwed on the wrong way, how was it I had no recollection of him when he was the wee fellah who worked at Number Twelve here . . .

Even the flashing of her eyes has dimmed: the socket, at times, seems to swim with that pale-blue, the pigment of the iris discolours in those pits of death, and I did not want to leave it at that but add, yes, of course, I remember now, just fancy, what a catastrophe, and the coffee begins to steam and gurgle on the stove, the most incredible coffee in the world that she alone knows how to make like this, weak beyond belief, she had even developed a hunch-back I imagine, as she bends to look for the oven-cloth to grip the handle of

the percolator, as if the back of her neck had con-
tracted, in the last month, so I say to her with a tinge
of our Lombard dialect:

'And how's yourself now?'

And I stared at those two fine lines, as she came up
to me with a steaming coffee-cup. They were like a
wound, showing dissolution just where I would have
least expected.

Nothing was asked of me: I stirred two or three
times, and I was already on my way.

And yet there must be a chink, a crack which you
can put your eye to and look. I felt it my duty to find
Her, I had time enough to do it, and now five hundred
thousand lire ('pay bearer'), advanced to me on the
strength of the contract. In fact, I was astounded to
discover that I had never thought about it before, if
you except the occasions determined by the passing of
some relative. Not one friend of mine had been torn
from me in youth. The drab adolescence I passed
through had chased away even the shade of Her.

But now I wanted to know, probe, investigate, make
myself ready.

Meanwhile it was misty: I could make out, and no
more, the white boundary wall of the sports ground,
a familiar sight, of Giuriati Park, the music which had
accompanied my steps at first had suddenly stopped,
big holes have broken the crust of the bricks at man
height, a foot or two below the inscribed stone which
I now saw superimposed in some lightning film effect,
the stone inscribed with our ten names, and I stood
there straining every nerve in the attempt to control my

terror, to hide the trembling which was shaking me inside, and the acute belly pain which bent me double made me fix them in the eye, one by one, the mere boys making up the squad, I searched their gazes, I trusted in their quite ordinary faces, they were not capable of such an irrevocable act, but they never look until the end, and then it is past the 'v' of their rifle-sights, they rested their boots on the edge of the track, touching the hard ground, one or two stamped with the cold, the terraces were deserted, the sergeant clapped his two gloved hands over his ears, then brusquely threw his arms wide again, everything seemed too paltry, the setting too trivial to be the one specifically chosen — an error of judgement we shall all fall into, when the moment comes — and Emilia stood away to one side with a little group of men in overcoats, as if she did not see me, when the chaplain began to walk towards us, I was the first in line and I wondered what to do, I saw his violet-coloured stole heaving on his breast, one or two in our line had already fallen to their knees, give me time, I said, if I could drink a glass of water first, and his hand advanced in benediction, committing me before I had decided, before I had pronounced any fitting words, or said a last farewell to everything that was there before me: the fur collar which set off Emilia's pallor, her cork heels, breath smoking in the mist, the white-wood caskets, with the lids removed, which I had noticed at the entrance, nothing but a shameful uneasiness; Emilia, I murmured, not crediting her indifference, and the anguish mounts, coming right up from the guts, begins to tighten at the neck, and yet you must keep a dry eye, at this very moment when some one of our number has burst out sobbing, sorry that he ever played the hero, and who would not be, if suddenly he has no control over his bowels, after dreaming a chance of greatness, spurred by his reading, ego te absolvo, says the breath in the mist, and I am crushed under a huge weight, shame for others and for myself, fully aware that Emilia would not lift a finger, I heard the bolts crashing home, I wondered which chamber was loaded with blanks, clinging to the last shreds of cowardice, I begin to count the seconds, one should shout something, an undying phrase, and now I know how ridiculous it is, unless it is to give you courage, I shall count more slowly, seven, eight, nine, after one last glance at the crumpled profiles of my fellows, you should relax your muscles so that they offer the minimum of resistance to the volley, on my flesh I can already feel the first stones thrown, but it is the officer's revolver shot ('to be sure') that horrifies me most, the body's last puppet twitching, and finally the voice said, singling me out, and it was Doctor Y giving orders:

'No, this, no. Not this one.'

Bad news reaches me by post, good news over the phone. No matter when I walk up to the little instrument, I never feel the anxiety I do in lifting an envelope. There is optimism in the ringing that opens the day; even when there is a bore at the other end of the line, you are made to feel you have some power in the world. So I lunged from the shower and grabbed the receiver, I recognized Ric's voice, a circle of drops formed almost at once on the floor, my whole forearm protruding from the sleeve of Emilia's bath-robe, my feet now surrounded by a little moat, fine, I said to Ric, we'll meet tomorrow for lunch.

I went out on the balcony, the clearness of the air took my breath away, a breeze was combing the sky out, towards north-north-east. There are things which I shall never verify for myself: if it is really true that the tawny owl hoots, and the teal rasps and scops owl whoops, and the blackbird whistles, and the thrush trills: at any rate the sparrows were singing all at once on things which, for brevity's sake, we shall call trees, because not even Emilia has ever managed to find out what kind they are: a sulky chirping that Luigino the caretaker has tried to drown, for a whole hour together, with the racket of his mower.

Waiting for me, clamped to the portable's roller, was Chapter One, the light streaming through the wide open french windows blotted out the bed, the imprint of our bodies, did away with even negligible shadows. I lit a cigarette, fell back on the chaise-longue, putting off decision, I lay there listening to the clang of scaffolding tubes being unloaded from a lorry, where a block, alive with bee-like workers, is rising up beyond the dead cars in the wrecker's yard, a back-cloth of clear sky, or one with only light cloud, along the whole sweep of the Alps, two-eighths of strato-cumulus over the Market, thermal zero at a thousand feet, which adds up to the state of perfect contemplation.

In that state I began to wonder what Ric was after: probably he had heard. The figure of Doctor Y who had witnessed my abject surrender began to take on the look of an enemy. Someone had told on me. And if Ric was informed about it, what he would say was only too clear.

'Anyone who, with a view to selling or distributing them, or publicly exhibiting them, makes, imports, purchases, possesses . . .'

Here Ric's voice would pick up speed in reading this clause of the law.

'. . . exports or circulates obscene writings, drawings, images, or other obscene objects of any kind, is liable to a period of imprisonment of from three months to three years . . .'

He would snap the penal code shut with his gaze still searching mine: he was on the point of saying (he would say this, for sure) that if I had needed money, I should have come to him, seeing that Article 528 fixes from three months to three years, and here there is no exemption for 'works of art', do you see what you are mixed up in?

A plane drew a trail on the blue from east to west.

Of course I saw what I was mixed up in: pure pornography. I could have put the blame on Emilia for not forbidding me such a crime. On the other hand, experience of prison which they describe as fundamental, could have given me a new way of looking at the world.

I began to wonder where I had lived through this moment before, so great was the void engulfing me: a fly motionless on the white of the sheets, the awareness that there was no need for me to write anything new except the one hundred and fifty typescript pages, double-spaced, which Doctor Y would find suitable illustrations for.

The breeze still blew, it erased thoughts just as they were taking shape, I savoured my discontent without trying to discover the reasons for it, because they, whatever they were, never stopped tormenting me under the layer of indifference and healthy cynicism with which we bury such matters. I refused to consider them boldly, so as not to have to alter my vision of things in the slightest particular. But even dreams leave scars. If I closed my eyes, I sank into nausea at myself, nausea at my past, there was little not to be ashamed of. I was invaded by a malaise, a brute impatience with what I had been compelled to accomplish and which I had accomplished nonetheless with a will, by a mood of doubt that called in question even the solidity of material objects, the knowledge that things too were wearing away, the dust collecting on books, the perishing of dry flowers, of velvet, of carpets, the minute crumbling of ceilings, of plaster, the disease in bricks which a blade of sunlight opens up in all its deadly course.

Then the flute, with the sharpest interval between one note and the next. Two hands covered my eyes: Miriam, I exclaimed. Now the liquid ran in the vein, they rubbed my arm, generating a sensation of warmth. You're good, they said. Like that. Again. And once more I sink my fingers in two snail-shells, it seems, with a trembling that invades brain and then body, a vibrating note of four hundred hertz, and although its intensity does not vary, it ends by assaulting the ear with a series of crescendi, that your anguish fears must terminate in an explosion.

Don't stop, they said together. I did not see their faces which were covered by their skirts lifted right up to their eyes, but I knew it was Miriam by her hoarse panting, she who had never let herself go with a girl friend there, while the waiters, busying themselves about the tables, moved nearer and nearer in menace, I know that I was falling, the carnations, the long, slender vases blurring to the eyes, terrified by such naturalness, swallowed up once again by the two of them as in some miracle, a painting that takes on flesh and with anguish I looked at nothing, breathed in nothing, chained to those blood-red clefts, edge of the whirlpool, my weakness provoked them and then drew back on the lip of the proffered entry, those flaming gullets, I could not see their faces but both women were overcome, excitement flushing Miriam from neck to temples, her irresistible moan, they sunk my fingers in without the least repugnance, made them follow out a horrifying path, and the beyond which the imagination pictures as made up of mouths opened wide in chorus, great spaces and horizons, of treble voices above a bass of anathema, raised up new roots, orifices, blades of flesh, in a quaking of petals and pistils, of knives and sudden cold dawns, and all the afterlives man has invented to keep his courage up, flashed simultaneously in that likeness. Now, they gasped, come now.

'Not bad. But let's try the service again.'

The instructor made off to gather up the balls scattered along the foot of the wire netting. In spite of the cool autumnal weather, I was bathed in sweat after that half hour's play. I do this for Emilia who finds her best relaxation in tennis, just so that, one day, I may be able to return her strokes decently.

Like this, the instructor repeated: left foot in line with the ball. I shall never succeed in capturing Emilia's ease, the agility of her strokes, her natural abandon, you're all tensed up, she scolds, learn to relax, lower that shoulder, and I comply without real conviction. (When she is the one returning, it is not balls she sends over so much as these curt little messages, don't stand so stiffly, darling, this is an English game, she speaks even when she is hitting a backhand, and at every contact of her racket there is the clean report of a bottle being uncorked, so different from the sound I make).

'Ten minutes more,' he says, glancing at his watch.

He bends down and uses his racket to draw back two balls that have passed under the net, the sun had risen and now shone on the orange-plastered façade of the Nerve Hospital, the white frames of the pavilions, the domes of the university, it poured light on the dead leaves of this false, Scandinavian-type city, the railway embankment, haunts of childhood, much loved though they have no special charm.

'That's better now,' he said. 'Just watch how you move your body.'

Out of a life we should save at least four or five images. Yet even those will go, leaving faded negatives, blurred shadows, and they must have removed the sound-track, because my racket strikes without a sound, at the windowsills of the Nerve Hospital, two heads show and watch us, limp wraiths come to witness our triumph of muscular skill, ghosts in flannel pyjamas glimpsed by a child with anguish, they are immediately called away by a nun or a jailer, the smell of disinfectant is exhaled from open windows, I had never seen any connection and now everything links up, is related, depends, their remote gaze lost upon this red-sanded court, their being aware that this is their last viewpoint, and then gauze bandages, the urine tubes, the incinerators, cries drowned by the expresses' hoot, there will be nothing then, the small voice says, nothingness, you know?

I wondered how Emilia could never have thought of it. And not my mother either, nor Ric, nor Doctor Y, nor the friends one confides in. And, also, if this voice (which I began to distinguish as progressively less mysterious and more and more real) were a sudden disorder of the brahmarandhra, the hollow of Brahma which we unbelievers call the cerebellar hemispheres.

In fact I threw down my racket.

'I've had enough,' I told the instructor.

He smiled like an Easterner, his lips unparted, and only then did I notice that he had the slant eyes and bronzed skin of a Bodhisattva. It struck me as a promising sign. Perhaps I am still in time, I thought.

From the hospital windows my silent watchers had vanished.

I have never wanted to believe that there are events which decide for us, but now clear signs, each one more telling than the last, were shaking my great confidence; they urged me to detach myself from appearances, to direct my gaze beyond the surface of things, to where the warnings are encountered which some one, who is to remain unknown, has set out with minute care.

As if the beam from a lighthouse were sweeping by, the image of Her would be lit up and then, at once, blacked out again: a brief flash in the dark that seemed to let me — (the petrol lorry coming straight towards me bulked larger and larger) — catch Her glance almost, be the only one to recognize Her just as the trailer passed, shaking the road at the level of my gaze, one of the tyres smeared with blood, a clot of feathers, and then it sped into the distance, carrying away even the illusion that I had glimpsed Her, looked Her in the eye if only for a second.

I could be mistaken: that is the opinion in these cases. Unhurriedly I mounted the pavement. But in the lift, just as I was pressing the button for the seventh floor, I was struck by the sight of that hand of mine: it was too grown up, almost as if it had grown old on its own account. It is strange to think how, until I was thirty, these hands of mine inspired me with so little confidence. And now maturity has given them a strength that never ceases to amaze me when I have to call on it, something I must tell Emilia: have you noticed how the skin on the back seems glazed with the years, and how the veins stand out more, the fingers grown thinner, or, to be more exact, bony and lean from use, hands that have become perfect servants of our every pleasure, only, on the back you can survey a relief-map of age, of wrinkles from wrist to joints, a network which time enriches with ridges and channels.

'I'm behind with things,' Emilia informs me from our little kitchen. 'I'll rush you up something.'

She had come back at midday, already tired out; a tinge of disappointment shows through her make-up: a patient she has been attending for two years now, a woman separated from her husband, who, since their little boy's death, has been quite alone, has tried to kill herself. Perhaps it was because of this that I felt guilty at enjoying the shower so much, after my tennis.

You know, I wanted to say to her, a little while ago, in the avenue, just outside . . . Well? . . . Nothing: I seemed to catch a glimpse of Her. And I would add:

blood and feathers, perhaps the guts of it . . . But are you sure?

During these six years that we have lived together, we have often had these dialogues, with me writing the lines for both voices. However, the line she comes out with now, just as we are sitting down to table, takes me completely off guard.

'You coming with me to Paris on Thursday?'

And she should know that we are hard up, that it is precisely for that reason that I have signed the contract with Doctor Y, and moreover I would have to put off my engagement with Ric, give up four days' work.

'Come on, make up your mind.'

I know I shall yield in the end: we have not been to Paris for years, last time was when we went to take in the Surrealist exhibition, and it would give me the chance to meet Edo, to shake off these nightmares about Miriam, and, lastly, to nip all these unanswerable questions in the bud.

'Well, then?'

The blame for this lies with the pop song in the background, Federico's Ballad Number One, which drags you down, drags you down, just when you were about to rise, with a simple phrase repeated *ad infinitum*, while the right hand extemporizes; why not leave everything as it is? the piano suggests, but then you do not understand, the refrain puts in, that life is this once, until the roar of the jet-liner drowns every other sound, it was a moment of weakness, nothing, it has passed: and here is the aircraft pointing its way above nurseries, whirring majestically over the roofs of Lambrate, in an hour we are at the airport of Orly.

Emilia was still holding the sheaf of notes she had prepared for the congress on her knees, I felt as carefree as a tourist, in rising up behind the other passengers who were cautiously filing through the exit, and I went along shedding my remorse for not having stayed at home to work. By noon we were in our hotel, we went out for lunch, then, outside the restaurant, separated. Emilia hailed a taxi, we were to meet up again later, at the hotel.

'Are you going to the concert?' were her parting words through the window.

'I don't know,' I said, 'but, remember, I expect you to shine.'

I walked on, going nowhere in particular. I was the master of Paris. I came out at Seine-side, at the Pont de la Conciergerie, I leaned over the parapet. The river flowed by, swollen but smooth, it almost lapped the signal poles on the bank. It had rained for days and now a brisk wind blew. Slowly I made my way towards the book-stalls: I caught sight of their dark-green projections all along that stretch of embankment, I had always loved this city, would have chosen to live there, and now, for the first time, her beauty struck me as wanton, as aggressive, even against the grey of a cloudy sky, or perhaps just because of that, the waning gilt of the gates, the bridges swept clean by the autumn breeze, attic windows and gardens laid out in their unchanging order, and I asked myself if it was not this being perfect as a painting which hurt me, the city's semblance of being eternal which rose up against my first, faint notion of Her: a challenge.

'Would you like something better?'

The man who spoke to me wore a beret and a black smock, he waved to the prints which I was absentmindedly glancing through. I said no thank you, and he went back to his seat by the parapet, but still kept an eye on me. The wind rustled the edges of these coloured sheets, flowers, landscapes, seduction pieces, old battles, clipped above the stall, and on the stall itself the usual books wrapped in cellophane, promising excitement as you worked through them with a paper-knife, series that were dear to Doctor Y and which I would perhaps have been wise to dip into myself, seeing that I was about to add a text of my own to them, keep that character, the married woman, will you, said Doctor Y, and yet there is something romantic in the declared secrecy of the wrappings, so there I was lingering over these volumes, I judged their bindings and their spines while my indifference steadily diminished, I wondered how all these productions still found buyers nowadays, when the tourist in Copenhagen can buy any of the positions from the postcard racks.

'Seventy francs,' said the man from behind me.

I dropped the book I was holding and moved off. I had taken about half a dozen steps and a youth comes up beside me, he says, as if he were talking to himself: would you like to see something out of the ordinary, guaranteed to thrill, I mean, a couple of Lesbians?

I had fallen for that one in London, on Greek Street, where they had lifted five pounds from me to see 'two Lesbians in bed', and so I crossed over to the opposite pavement, even although it amused me to think of myself trying that sort of entertainment at the very moment when Emilia was sitting at the opening session of her congress, with the headphones on, to follow some delegate's speech in translation. But here was I at Paris and I could have been anywhere, I went along those streets, through squares, museums, forgetting her meanwhile, I let myself go with the current that swept along by the Seine right to Chaillot, I walked round the Musée du Costume, losing myself among the dummies spotlit against backcloths of red velvet, against black velvet drapes, the effect of them was somewhat chilling as if they formed a material catalogue to a kind of writing which I had cherished, and it is here that old ladies today bring their grand-children, in this self-same Paris, to see Odette Swann in her wedding dress, *grandes dames* attended by pages, stepping down from a carriage for the gala, in the sixteenth district, and they study the dummies, and the dummies look elsewhere as if to spare themselves the implications of all those stares.

I, too, was elsewhere inside half an hour; I was standing in the Musée d'Art Moderne, before Matisse's 'Buffet Vert', and the attendant had dozed off on the couch, his peaked cap nodding forward, amid the stamping of feet come here from a good half of Europe, I do not remember what I was looking for in that smell of waxed floors, by the oblique shafts of light, at any rate the tea-room of the Café de la Paix was steadily filling, old ladies cutting their pastries under the gilt-stuccoed ceiling, I have always been touched by this spectacle which is to be enjoyed in there, from the region of the biscuit counter, with the taste of the chocolate you have been drinking still in your mouth, and the cake trolley near to hand, so much so that I did not notice how time was passing.

Now the great slate-sombre dusk was falling, with wings and trophies in bronze, raised against the sky which a starry wind tore open. From the boulevards came the first twinklings: suddenly I remembered Edo.

I had a good two hours at my disposal before Emilia would get back to the hotel. A bus went by. The wind filled out the awning at a corner café. I tried to master my own throbbing excitement, now that I was deciding on an expedition that prudence warned against.

In my notebook I found his address but no telephone number. After all, our acquaintance had come about through our corresponding. But his name was not to be found in the telephone directory either, and this led me to think that Edo had never existed outside of the letters he sent me, long, extraordinary letters, to the last of which I had not yet replied.

'Square Jean Davaux,' I told the taxi-driver.

He himself had to trace the place first on a map of the city. My uneasiness grew. Only natural, Emilia would have explained, it is the unrest produced by even the smallest departure from our code of behaviour, unwritten laws govern our decisions, and so I felt myself part victim and part hangman, less and less certain that I was performing an act of reparation, until after half an hour's journey a jumble of habitations and courtyards blocked our way.

'The square is in there,' the driver informed me.

A clearing all of concrete, dim little lights over the entries to staircases, a porter's room lit only by television images, then a tiny, all-metal lift right up to the sixth floor, a visiting card nailed to the first door on the left.

With my second ring a fairy with blued hair appeared on the threshold. I asked for Edo: she lowered her eyelids and left me to an enormous cat, I glimpsed a little, dark hallway, some one had struck chords from the lower register of a piano, the cat stared at me, wide-eyed, from the end of the hallway a voice sang out, but it can't be, now this is a surprise.

And then I saw Edo.

He was tall and angular, as I had imagined, but with a silk scarf at his neck and his white hair combed carefully. I was natural, on my side too, in embracing him.

'Denyse,' he called out. 'Guess who's come?'

I followed him along a narrow corridor lined with books, to the room the chord sequences were coming from. The fairy who had opened the door for me was giving a music lesson to a boy. The pupil was at once dismissed, a steaming tea pot appeared in our midst, Denyse's short arms were of the whitest, her smile like a queen's.

'You're just like your photograph, isn't that true, Denyse, isn't he exactly the same?'

I flushed, already won over to what they had in mind, and, as it turned out, they had decided that I must stay to dinner, and in the meantime answer a hundred questions, the cat had leapt up onto Edo's knees, and I watched his hand scratching the animal's throat as he spoke to me of my novels with a familiarity which deepened my embarrassment, Denyse agreed every now and again with a benign nod, there was a strong odour of dust exhaled by the carpet, the blood-red cover on the bed, the assembled piles of books, perhaps by the piano itself, yet I felt a prisoner, unmindful even of Emilia and every obligation, I sank down into that quiet talk, into a little universe of framed photographs of the illustrious, steaming cups and the butts of gauloises, we soon found we shared enthusiasms for particular works and people, so that an hour was enough to lay bare our weaknesses and blind spots, Denyse meanwhile had begun to lay the table with crystal goblets and a silver dinner service.

By that time Emilia must have come to the end of

her session, she would not have found me back at the hotel for the hour we had agreed on.

'Why not ring her up and ask her to join us?'

Edo was now asking what I was working on, and I realized I could not lie to him: but of course, he smiled, even a filthy book can have its value if it is written by a writer, and you know it, you who can go far, you are one of the few, only, nothing must frighten you, perhaps you lack courage, do you follow me?

I listened to him ecstatically, though at moments I was hemmed in by the fear that he might sense other things in me, detect something to disappoint him, like the question that I carried deep down and that I wanted to put to him as soon as he mentioned his health. But instead of that he told me he had fought with the militia at Tarragona, he asked me whose company I kept at Milan, what I thought of Ric and his publishing house, but with no great interest, merely as if he were putting together a case history for his own use.

In the room misty with cigarette smoke his face stood out clear in the lamplight, from the kitchen came the aroma of onion soup: good cooking, he said, matters, and love, politics, literature, God, how many passions there are for a life that is so short, that is why you need the courage to choose, to jettison the super-fluous at once, I did not miss a word he said, we were moving close in feeling, and in the event it was he who reminded me that I had still to get in touch with Emilia.

I rose up and went to the phone: she had just got back, with a splitting headache, so she would rather go straight to bed. We sat down to table. A vague disappointment was all they expressed. It was clear that, on this first occasion, they had not wanted to share me even with Emilia. Denyse let me know that, just the week before, the leading philosopher of present-day Germany had sat in the place I was occupying, at the head of the table, she said they all had a great liking for Edo, but Edo was a recluse, and she addressed this remark to me with a womanly ambiguity that disturbed me, or perhaps it was only the effect of the acquavite that, to round off an exquisite meal, Edo kept pouring into my glass. I was heated and anxious, as if this were the eve of some ceremony with a ritual of which I knew nothing at all.

'I don't follow, Edo, what sort of courage?'

Creakings traversed the ceiling, as if some one were watching us from up there, crouched in a corner, the cat had left us to curl up in the middle of the bed, Denyse took my hand and murmured if I preferred another kind of drink, there was something motherly and at the same time suggestive in her manner, but Edo seemed to approve.

'That was Schumann you were playing, wasn't it?'

Her face shone with pleasure, and while Edo was descanting to her on my love of chamber music, I tried to draw, out of their words, the real hard sense in them, they had both grown strangers to me now, remote, people the mind had not allowed as possible, any more than it could credit the existence of the hands which, from time to time, Denyse stretched out to him, across the table, displaying them like flowers that had just budded, and a dark and terrible dispensation brooded on us, and I was right at the centre of something I was not to forget, I found myself wondering what hid behind these two, behind the mystery of those so innocent gestures, behind the smell of the velvet, dust, paper, too much paper and cat urine.

'We're poor, you know, we've shaken off everything.'

It made me happy to believe him, to believe that they were really so, that there were people in the world like them, and that they loved me.

'Or, rather, we have never possessed anything, we've only shaken off the craze for possessing . . .'

At this point I was afraid that he might tell me about the two of them, of what they could do, he and Denyse, after all these years, I was afraid because I know what senile lust is like, how completely the old abandon themselves, with their shameless revelling in pleasure, the first knocking of the shutter in the wind was heard, better close them, he said to her, and at once there came a break, we both watched the slim, braceleted arms of Denyse stretching out in the dark to close either leaf, it could have been the beginning of a seance, the table still cluttered with the dishes, real characters and interpreters came the voice, and I was shut inside a romantic plot in three acts, a prisoner with no way of escape from the scarlet bed-cover which trailed to the floor, I was sure that the hanging on the wall concealed a horizontal mirror, perhaps it would open like a theatre curtain at the right moment, Edo spoke of totality, of how we should approach our work, every one of us, and I listened to him, horrified to think that I would not rise up no matter what was to happen now, but you're not drinking, he said, pouring me another acquavite.

The echo of our talk drifted over the glasses, the creaking from the ceiling accentuated large blanks of silence, Denyse was standing behind his chair, the hands she had rested on his shoulders slid gently down

37

towards his chest, two fingers slipped inside his shirt, his head to one side in an oriental posture, and he kept his eyes on me across that petrified interval: you never free yourself from it, he murmured, never, you understand that?

But the end, Edo? this was what urged itself on me. What will become of us, I wanted to ask him.

His left elbow rested on the table, right near the edge, and at its side stood the empty coffee cup, in a moment he was going to send it crashing to the floor, I could see that, yet I knew I was not going to stop him, not having it in me to break the spell of that uncanny hour with a stupid warning, now that Denyse has sat herself at the piano, the tones her hand raises from the bass, volumes of melody take shape, waver, begin to shift, Edo had stayed where he was, motionless as a Buddha, no stir in him except for the little beat where the silk scarf wound his throat, he willed me to look at him but I was watching him through Denyse now and through Denyse the very uneasiness that emanated from him still reached me, the wind shrilled at a gap in the shutters, its whistle rose higher in a rest during the second movement, then died altogether.

'You should see her naked,' he murmured, his eyes two glittering slits. 'She has the body of a girl.'

There in that room we seemed to be on the edge of a revelation.

Denyse must have heard him, her hands froze on the keys, she turned her queenlike smile on me and asked: 'Will you come back to the square?'

It was the crash of the little cup that shook us, but no one lowered their gaze to the fragments.

We were at the end of a concert, dazed in the void between the last note and the outbreak of clapping.

Midnight was near, Emilia would be asleep, I felt I should wake her, tell her the whole of it, but I already knew I would manage only a part.

We went down by foot, stair after stair, his hand running quickly along the banister of old wood. At the entrance I noticed that Edo was not nearly as tall as he had looked to me at table.

'The underground is at the end of the road: take the Châtelet line.'

I wondered if we would ever meet again.

I am wakened this morning by the water running in the wash-basin right behind my head, and, as I lie there, the noise of it flowing in the pipes is accompanied by a strange tinkling of metal on glass, the clash of little bottles that comes through the wall, a pause, Emilia is getting ready to go out, her frantic step and her 'see you later' thrown over her shoulder as she exits: what's the weather like? Stay put because it's cold.

The light from the hall fell on the case for an instant: not yet opened. It will stay like that until tonight when Emilia comes in and I shall help her to put out our clothes again, the shoes she wore to the restaurant, a shirt of mine I did not need, pointless items of dress which memory, in linking them to a gesture, a landscape, is already making immortal.

Over and above this, Emilia has taught me that we find the answers we are looking for precisely in the past, the true account of our present, and also the reasons for the mistakes we are still to make. A shame that her dogmatic way — we discussed this on the train, without understanding one another—prevents her from making any original suggestions on this head. Obsessions, she repeats, typical of a wealthy society. I wonder, however, if she is not just dead to the question. You know what you strike me as? she laughed at me, a retired colonel.

From the landing came the buzzing of a floor-polisher, I rose and, to cut off the noise, shut the bedroom door. In the few days we have been away a film of dust has settled on the phone. Every time we get back from a journey, I see this plain existence Emilia and I lead as the only one possible. I looked at the morning outside the window without the least notion of what time it was, I knew that I should work but also that I had no desire to. I dialled Ric's number and at once the engaged signal beeped. At times I think up wonderful projects like collecting nonsense rhymes, planting out a herbarium, ordering all the materials needed, but the little space we have chosen to live within always dissuades me from going ahead. Today I could look on this ability to slip my responsibilities as a final warning, a sort of wise recall that came to me from another continent.

'He's in conference,' his secretary answered.

'Call me back as soon as he's free.'

In the meantime, I told myself, stepping into the bath, there should always be signs with Beware written on them, placed just where She is most likely to appear, so you can be on your guard, like Beware blasting, or falling rocks, or Beware race-horses, only, then you would want to know how to react in the wretched eventuality of the mine's really blasting your way, and the rocks' breaking off and beginning to roll, and the thoroughbred's bursting free from its horse-box and galloping along the street, but in that case there should be placards hanging from the sky when the foulness of the air announces, like this morning, low cloud thick with poison. Too many notices admittedly, with a name on them that no one likes to see written out, unless it is on a theatre bill or the girders of a high voltage pylon.

I drew the plug from its socket, put down the razor and immediately heard a child crying on the stairs, now I could finish dressing and come down gently on to the pavement outside, ready for a stroll, a coffee at the tobacconist's counter, displaying my scorn of danger as I crossed a road junction which had no traffic-lights.

I was just about ready when Ric's voice sounded over the phone, he had just come out of a long meeting, however he was going on to Zurich that night, we could meet for lunch.

This appointment contented me. Lines of traffic moved forward, both ways, along the avenue, a trail of black smoke above the roof tops signed a take-off just that moment effected, at a first floor window a woman was beating a carpet, my little universe fell into place again: the newstand in line with the row of bare trees, the spiderweb of the gasworks, the yellowish façade in Via Zama, the Market, the minute houses of people come from the South.

Ric awaited me in another Milan, one more like him, of marble, crystal and soft arm-chairs.

'How far on are you with your work?'

I was ready to lie to him on this score: for two years now he has been expecting a novel from me that I have not even begun to write. And I could not tell him about my contract with Doctor Y, about the

41

weakness I had been driven to by an imperious need of cash.

'I've been to Paris with Emilia.'

We were in the usual restaurant he goes to for his business lunches. Just to see Ric invigorates me as much as his efficiency itself does, his aggressive way, the cut of his suit. I had made up my mind to tell him everything, or at least everything about that dominant thought; and here was his vitality infecting me. Even the sparse meals he takes are part of a programme, braced as he is at every moment for his personal battle with the world.

'Too bad about the other day, your English publisher was here, he wanted to meet you.'

I pointed out that his was no loss, I spoke to Ric of our brief trip, then of Edo.

'Did you look him up?'

He went on to say that, as far as he knew, Edo was a phoney, to cultivate him, a waste of time, in fact he did not understand what the devil I saw in him.

'That's strange,' I said. 'He made a tremendous impression on me.'

Ric was in the act of signing to the waiter to bring coffee. He broke off the gesture and stared at me pointedly: 'Is it to discuss him that you wanted to see me?'

To be honest, I did not understand this animosity, sprung from motives I did not care to discuss. I changed the subject, we ended up talking of trifles. Undoubtedly Ric (and here was something at least I could envy in him) was the last person to ask himself the question for which I vainly sought an answer. We stayed there another ten minutes, both distracted, then Ric paid the bill and we rose up.

'Let me see something of you,' he as good as

ordered, keeping hold of my hand. 'One of these Sundays I'll take you up for a flight.'

The chauffeur was waiting for him on the pavement, I admired Ric for his unshakeable tenacity, and also for his agility in throwing himself back on the rear seat, his flashing smile after a conversation he had not relished.

'I'll let you know how I get on,' I answered, speaking through the open window.

Once back home, a sense of frustration drove me to write the first ten pages of the damned book that Doctor Y expected two months from then.

I know it is the instinct of self-preservation that prompts our sorriest decisions. But I was not able to rid myself of it, not even with Emilia's help. I knew perfectly well the point I should have struck at, but I did not have the strength to, I looked for an alibi every time, I invented good reasons. We have no money, I told her. Something that is almost always true, but not enough to damn your immortal soul, or so she maintains, especially if we are lying, side against side, on the bed, like this evening, the room dark but for the television glow.

'Go on,' she invited.

In the confessional, as a boy, I was tongue-tied at the beginning in this selfsame way. And not knowing how common those terrible doings of mine were, I used to keep the worst to the last. Emilia must understand that too, for her caress is encouraging.

'I don't know how to put it: a kind of need to abase myself.'

'Anything more?'

It is strange that I had never chanced to think of it before, I mean as an eventuality that touched me personally. Now I was conscious that even as I strove to translate it into words, a wiser-than-thou tone crept into my voice (and quite false it was), leaving Emilia no room for her diagnosis.

'And this is what frightens you?'

I had called it need of money and instead it was a fear, a covered-up dread that she would never have understood, considering how different the patients are who attend at the Centre, with their reports of anxiety states and phobias that are much more obvious and classifiable, and it was only at this point that I could appreciate how privileged, how aristocratic, this type of premonition I was experiencing was, and, leaving aside the fanatical devotion which inspires the deeds of saints, how impossible to induce without a minimum of well-being.

An outbreak of sighs unite us, in pensive mood, until the next question.

'Is it because of what Edo said to you?'

That too, I say, but probably I knew all along: it is not the first time I have stood facing the gun muzzles, nothing wrong with that, according to her, a desire for punishment, perhaps an unconscious need of expiation, there must be some traumatic experience, transgression in youth, at the root of it, do you not remember? no, I don't remember, I had vowed to myself that I would speak to her about it with complete honesty: I keep thinking of it, Emilia, of course, she would answer, everyone is afraid, in her you meet with an almost physiological incapacity to treat a question as personal and particular, but I wasn't asking

44

you what you think about the spread of Esperanto, we are talking about ourselves, about our end upon this earth, and again she urges: go on, ah, that's it: to make love with a revolting creature, I think it was the girl in the news-stall down there on the corner, but with a superb body like Ric's secretary, figure of the goddess, how is that to be explained? it is to be explained once more as a longing for self-punishment, at bottom it could be a deviation of the masochist type, and we both laugh gently, only, Emilia abruptly stops, she seems disturbed, her hand is arrested between my third and fourth rib, pensively, and there is an exquisite moment as the needle trembles halfway between intellect and the senses, the blood swells our caverned bodies, a noticeable faintness in the voice, my victory now is if I can infect her with these revived emotions of mine, confuse her, involve in my malaise, go on until I have wrenched the first moan of pleasure from her, punish her for having dared to stand with telescope on the fray like the Emperor at Austerlitz, uncertain about throwing in the reserves, and you liked her, you liked her while you did it, is that it?

An obscure excitement possessed us, although it was still in our power, at that stage, to check it if we wanted: the television screen was a whirlpool that came nearer, that light it has, suggesting crime, poured on us inescapably, of course I liked her, I said, that is the strange thing in the circumstances, don't you think? I imagined Emilia agreed being on the point of succumbing, but, no, she came to herself suddenly, abruptly reminded of the theory expounded by the Master himself that civilization is to be identified with repression.

She blew out her lips, she propped up the pillow so that she could sit in a more upright position.

'Where were we?'

We were still caught in something not readily identifiable, that we could call the financial-anxious state but which now mattered little, just as what passed before our eyes itself mattered less and less: a train lying off the rails, police in some part of the world or other dragging along a man with bloody face, placards with slogans, generals at the airport, and Emilia murmured out of the blue: what are you thinking about?

She always has this look: with her bold profile turned to the windscreen, her lips hinting the bitter grimace to come, the knees smooth, the skirt that in another moment will slide right back to her groin, her thighs sunk in the soft leather of the seat. Or her shoes, her heels, her ankles, the unrivalled step she has as she comes up to the car from behind, a sound that by itself tells she has arrived.

'I was thinking of Miriam. You know, that girl.'

When Emilia telephones, as she has just done this morning, that she will not be back for lunch, I take refuge in a snack-bar: I mix with people who have just left work. So I slipped on my raincoat and went down to the bus stop. I let two overcrowded vehicles pass, then started off on foot under my favourite kind of sky, the neutral background which does not draw the passer-by's gaze, a greyness calculated to set off objects, the shape of things, people's faces, their breath, the tight lips of the straphangers, and I, too, upon my feet as I leant back against the car door, I was holding her hands to her side, Miriam yielded,

46

moving against me rhythmically, the moment to say goodnight had come, and, every time, the joy of her belly in another wave took my breath away.

I crossed the bridge: huge drills burrowed among pools, patches of damp showed through the tunnel walls, and on that strip of pavement that bordered the river of cars, Miriam walked ahead of me, rather she fled without running, making off, dazed, with her rapid step, foul-smelling trickles ate into the tar, I said to her, where are you going, try and understand, and I knew she would not turn round again, in fact I hoped she would not, a lorry had come down the ramp, and she would be at the end of the tunnel by this time, all that wrong, I thought, all that wrong for nothing, I felt her draw away from me, with her wound still warm, a dog overtook me, than a woman with a shopping bag, I was almost at the exit myself, other people hurried towards me, jostling, on the same pavement, they tried to come between me and the superb image of all her back laid bare which I was studying in the mirror, in the cold fury of a distant afternoon, her face that is a mass of hair, her childish shoulders which heave to the strokes, don't look, she begged, finally her weeping on my chest for joy, and from the end of the tunnel she is still crying out: don't look, but the roar of the motors drown her voice, the light scatters her ghost, the crowded square comes into sight, the avenue leading to Monforte.

'A coffee,' I ordered at the counter.

Emilia is right. I do squander my time. These wanderings which cut into working hours always drain me of energy. At times I would like to squat down on the pavement's edge and observe, through some

47

microscope, the bustling of the world, the life of my hectic city, people's faces.

All I did was to come out of the bar and let myself be carried along towards something which would take shape, as I went, as a necessary act. The music shop on the corner where the tube is stole a few moments of my time, but the record I was looking for was not to be found in that window, a recording of country sounds, and I was never going to find it. I would go and see my mother instead, as if I were going to make reparation, to meditate in pain, because I knew what would be awaiting me, when more than a month had passed since my last visit.

In the tube station I bought her a box of chocolates.

Going up those stairs, at every step I recover memories of grey years, of hardships. The garbage odour is the same, the worn doorsteps, the brass plate where his name is engraved has been covered by a white post-card bearing hers, her maiden one, the silence of the porters' room, the feeble light in the bare interior that has heard the country accent of generations. They have given a coat of varnish to the banister, painted the railings, and new plaster covers the main walls, but it does not hide the patches of dampness, the cobwebs, the smears on the floor that have escaped cleaning, traces of crushed insects, I know the exact places on the stairs, the marks gone into the steps' porous face. To have survived these transformations makes my mother legendary in some ironic way.

Each time, as she is giving me the brief hug of greeting, she seems tinier, her features, more wasted,

I feel I have to say at once, to make her happy.

'But what luxury you live in! — they've been decorating the stairs.'

Of course they have, she answers; then goes on to mutter it was high time. Her smile passes in a flash, but I know she is pleased. This should be the moment for talking to one another, as my cheek is leaving hers: I feel the wish come, then fade, unaccountably checked by the reticence which I first learnt from her.

'It's not as if it would kill Emilia to come with you just once!'

I explain that she is being kept terribly busy, that we have just got back from Paris, the required excuses that my mother lets pass without any comment at all.

'So you've smoked four cigarettes already,' I tell from the ash-tray, on the kitchen table.

She defends herself, glad that I am remonstrating with her, as no one will now.

'O no, you can put two down to Signora Bernotti, she came in this morning to borrow the paper.'

The kitchen is where we talk, the living room is for strangers. The word illness is never mentioned. And how are your troubles? I ask her in the casual tone I know she prefers.

The indifference on her side is just as assumed: for two weeks now she has managed to sleep at nights, so she has given up the cure. She turns her head away quickly, in case I might read other signs in her gaze. The truth is that I wanted to tell her how absorbed I myself had become in thinking of that day; I wanted to urge her not to be afraid because I knew every particular of her funeral as if it had taken place already, in a time previous to my existence and even to hers.

'Now your brother, he came last Sunday with the children.'

Undoubtedly she enjoys more relief with him, can play her part, even believe she will last out longer. Moreover I have always found it hard to discuss this with her. A string of average mishaps has taken away her hope in another, more perfect existence. The fault, she says, of my father who murdered her life.

'And now the price of milk has gone up, you must have read about it.'

I have not read about it, but this reminds me that I have also come to leave my monthly tribute, more of a token than anything else, a gesture in recognition of her struggle to raise me, of the time when she stayed up at night to make sure she could pay the rent, the sewing machine jarring on into the small hours obedient to her foot, and there was an empty place in the bed where my father would never stretch out again.

'One of these Sundays I'll come with Emilia and we'll take you for a run in the car.'

Tiredly she nods, she knows only too well that this is not going to happen, because, for too long now, her place has been within these four walls. Not even one thing in the room has been moved: on the old refrigerator, bulking too large in the corner, stand the selfsame adornments, a rearing horse, an embroidered table-centre, the alarm clock in the foreground, objects I came to hate in youth, the only recent additions being the photographs of her grandchildren, and a postcard from the seaside, 'greetings from Riccione', stuck into the glass door of the dresser.

Listen to me a moment, I should say to her.

She has slipped a cigarette from my packet with

impatient fingers, and I should say to her, listen, don't smoke so much, I know it's the only vice you have, apart from drinking coffee, but her coffee could not hurt a canary, and there is something birdlike about her, too, in the fineness of her drawn neck, in the little head that she impatiently shakes amid the smoke from the cigarette.

'I am thinking of letting your room,' she makes the admission with embarrassment. She is afraid that I will not like the idea of a stranger coming to sleep in my bed or in my brother's. It is a natural step to take, I tell her, a house is not a museum, after all, the one thing worrying me is the possibility that the cleaning will fall on her shoulders, on those transparent arms that hang down from her dressing-gown.

'At least I'll have something to do.'

'Yes, but, rather than that, you should go out. As soon as you feel better. To get some fresh air. You don't imagine it's doing you any good, to spend the whole day in front of the television?'

She has pulled a face, exactly as she would when she was a young miss, the selfsame expression is there in the photo-album, and this is to persuade me into thinking that she will last a long time yet; to suggest that I was making a mistake when hers, mine, our end had seemed so close that day I went down into the tunnel near the Market.

A look that brings her more alive than I have seen her for ages, at the very moment when I am searching for the courage to say, for all the years of married love not lived, of dry-eyed weeping, of sacrifice, the courage to say to her: you know, I am afraid that this illness, that you are going just like that, without having had anything, not even that cursed pension.

She had risen up to strike a match on the metal of the oven to light the gas-ring.

'Here's the money,' I said. 'See you soon.'

The most unbearable days when of all our simple acts not one seems worth the performing, especially if Emilia is standing before the balcony windows and the rain streaks the panes, the trees are swallowed up in the mist that presses everywhere, muffling the few cars that pass, deadened light bathes her face as it questions a sky that is no longer there, changed to a screen of water, sarabande, gigue, passacaglia, the well-ordered measures of a Sunday afternoon, with a commanding harpsichord that imposes silence.

Your Handel depresses me, she will say in a minute, could you not put on something else? I know how restive she is in suffering this climate, the sight of rain flowing, running along invisible joins, filling and rotting every crack.

'Come over here,' I said. 'You lie down too.'

She has crossed her arms, her head is sunk a little way into her shoulders, her brow, glued to the pane, her profile blurs on the curtain that falls behind her.

'I don't feel like sleeping,' she answered after a pause.

If it were an unending sleep you could fall into, it would be almost sweet, a reward. Instead of that, the nothingness of it is what we cannot bear, our knowing that we will be aware of nothing.

'One of these Sundays,' I said to her, 'would you like to come to the Necropolis with me?'

Without answering she has sat down on the bed,

looks for the lighter, the smoke is billowing out into the room, and now that the concerto is over, the silence menaces, assaults us with that boundless pleasure. Naturally there was not a great deal left for that moment: her step on the gangway, her ankle, calf, the flash from a film-still, none of the dear images that our fancy nourishes in moments of abandon. In place of that, the mirror of our own bewilderment, long minutes in which shameful fears are all that show there; phantoms which all have the one name now. Because, of so much trusting and struggling and hoping, nothing is left us but Her, the only certainty in a sea of doubts, the one truth among endless uncertainties, and so we should learn not to fear Her, to put away the superstitious regard they have instilled into us, never to mention Her by name, and for another good reason too: we have seen a time of slogans and loud trappings, an age in which She was mocked and laughed at, skull and crossed bones on caps and belts, hell and its flames, but all to little effect, and the scorn was only pretended.

'What's wrong, you in a sad mood?'

If there is one sort of question that will irk me, it is this sort, as Emilia well knows. We shall end up bickering, in fact, we have already begun, now that I have retorted, who knows why sadness – expressive word – is thought to be a shameful feeling. Not to mention the fact that there is a kind of cosmic sadness . . .

'What did you say?'

There is deliberate sarcasm in her look, as she sits, head turned over her shoulder at me, elbow resting on knee, cigarette poised in mid-air: I was not going to forget this study of her, in fact, I was already framing it for my gallery of unposed shots, an ironic gaze that was not giving way to motherly indulgence this time.

Because she has noticed for a while now that I am not myself, that I worry myself with pointless questionings, that I am wasting my time, withdrawing more and more into myself, into miserable fantasies.

'Now listen, Emilia . . .'

But I shall not succeed in communicating my sterile anguish to her, because she already meets with enough of that in her profession, and what I want to do is to shake myself, react, put myself to work but in earnest, not let myself drift, and, if anything, go out more, see people, bestir ourselves, even to the point of moving house, because we cannot go on living in a single room for ever, it may be romantic but an end will come and it is coming right now . . .

'You forget one thing,' I said.

Of course: that we have no money, she was a fury let loose, she seemed to be reading from a page or reciting something learnt by heart, barely restraining the violence which stems from her firm beliefs, and she went through them again, intoned a list of reproaches which humiliate us both, which, in any case, I had no desire to listen to.

'Let up, Emilia, for any favour.'

But money is there to be earned, that is not the problem, and without having to sell your immortal soul, as I was doing, only you need strength, that minimum of drive that I had lost, because the truth . . .

'Go on, say it, don't be afraid.'

She stubbed her cigarette-end in the ash-tray, with her eyes on me.

'The truth is that you can no longer write.'

I had forced myself on to my feet again, I did not exactly know what I was after, I almost staggered as I entered the bathroom, I looked at myself in the mirror, on my face, the mark of a whip-lash, I felt emptied of weight, cleaned out by some electric shock, I do not remember how long I stayed there like that; when I came out, Emilia was sitting on the edge of the bed again, deathly pale.

'Sorry,' she murmured.

This had never happened, or at least never with the violence that springs from hidden rancour. But I am not an easy one to live with, as I have always been the first to admit.

'That woman we were looking after: she killed herself last night.' After a pause she added: 'I suppose I don't count for much myself.'

But the madness that overflows from the television screen, from the newspapers, their very headlines, how could it strike at us, infect our sureness? Once more I went back to my question, with the feeling that I was going after something that had already dissolved in air, the ungraspable husk of a thought that was too high for me, too far from all I could touch, measure, interpret.

'I've read those thirty odd pages you've just written.'

It was the beginning of the book commissioned by Doctor Y. No point in her telling me what she thought of them.

'When?'

'A few days ago. I should have told you.'

My face burnt. I was caught in the act. I had to look away. The only thing I found to do was to stretch out on the bed again. But it was too soon to give in, later we would discuss it all calmly, for the moment I had to win back ground with her, at all costs put off my defeat.

Emilia let me seize her hand.

'Down here, at my side.'

I press against her shoulder gently, close your eyes, what do you see? nothing she answered, nothing? we are beside the sea, a beautiful sea, so calm, with little waves that go shhhk, a dazzling sun blazing down, tang of the salt, you know the breeze that you always feel on the shore, a pause, Emilia's shoes on the coverlet — exciting flashback to love play that had been paid for — on the coverlet with the toes of them brushing the curtain, the silence in the house today when mist has closed the airport, so let's get our imagination working, Emilia, I am not really finished, then: we are lying out, like this, on the foreshore, with the motion of the waves as they go and come right up to our knees, you are sinking your fingers in the damp sand, are there any bathers? no, there are none, they have all gone away for lunch, only the sound of the sea, shhhk, do you hear it now? I hear it; lovely; I get the smell of your sun-tan oil, breathe deep, there is nothing else, you and I alone in the blue, this is better, she smiles, it seems real, my hand meets the foam of her slip, goes up and then slides long, here is the wave now, be careful not to take too much sun, of course, she said, the sea, she gasped, the sea.

Every year in mid-January Ric and his wife gave a party to mark their wedding anniversary. I had managed to miss a few of them; this time Emilia was the one who took the call and she accepted the invitation.

Anyway, it was just as well for me to come out of my shell and renew contacts, when being out of harmony with the world—as Emilia maintains—is precisely what lacerates the individual psyche.

Ric and Francesca—as I was free to observe all over again, from my look-out post between drawing-room and library—had little enough to do with one another, and even that was superficial, but, in public, they liked to make a show of fondness, so that they passed for a model couple.

'Have you met that lady? Yes? Well, come and I'll introduce you to Anselmi then, come on, you can't skulk there.'

This meant I had to rise up and follow Ric, glass in hand. On these occasions Emilia travels from couch to couch like a butterfly, from one pale, boring group to another, picks up scandal, and starts little actions to further my career. Anselmi was standing beside a candelabra, surrounded by women, he shook my hand without even pretending interest. On my side I loathed him, although we had met that moment: he was the type of intellectual whom, when I was younger, I would gladly have seen hung, a sometime poet, then essayist, and now a newspaper editor, more cynical every day and ready to stoop to anything.

I was about to move away when a woman's arm, it was Francesca's, slipped through mine and forced me to stay, forced me, in fact, to wait for an example of Anselmi's wit which was greeted by laughter all round. It was followed by a killing pause, I asked Francesca to repeat the remark which I had missed.

'Darling, how are you?'

She was carried off at that very moment. But the savouries were excellent and so was the whisky. At the buffet table I came across Ric again, busy serving a magnificent girl, both were still shaking with mirth at Anselmi's latest sally.

'But never trust men who are too intelligent: in the end they come out with ideas that are just the opposite of ours.'

It pained me to see how greatly he admired him, because Ric is of a more honest kind, whereas Anselmi belonged with people who invariably take generosity, disinterested action, consistency, for stupidity pure and simple. Ric patted my shoulder with a knowing look, Emilia was signalling to me with her eyes to come over, I joined her and she introduced me to someone in television who immediately denied that he would love to screen versions of my short stories. In these matters Emilia was born yesterday, she believes the things that are said strictly to make conversation, she gave me a radiant smile, but I did not return it.

Two handsome ladies walked about with a distracted air, quite impervious to the charm of the great writers who stood apart in impenetrable confabulations, but it was the two ladies I envied for the age they had known, sure of its conventions and of its distinctive cultural shape. Waiters hired for the occasion urged their loaded trollies at the guests, words assailed me from all sides, I tried not to heed their meaning.

'It makes no difference,' they were saying, 'but you have to admit he has a sense of history.'

Do you know what a sense of history is? Emilia seemed fascinated by the question: I could not make her see that our history, too, so solidly there before us, was soon to pass. Now I could press a last whisky on myself, and, as I did so, catch the story a fashionable lady was telling her companion of how they, that was herself, the French military attaché, and a friend of the Ambassador's, had gone out in a helicopter to hunt tiger and it turns into a veritable manhunt across the jungle, something that would have made you die of excitement, and now she is going to Easter Island with two English newspapermen to solve the mystery of those stone heads.

I could not stomach whatever else was to come, perhaps an eye-witness account of how some negroes had been lynched. I signed to Emilia that it was time to go. I felt hot, the groups were formed now, the smoke curdled, I heard Anselmi saying: I've just been to Brioni, to visit Tito, such a charming man, lives like a pasha, then I noticed it was not Anselmi but a woman with a masculine look who stood at his side, because the trouble with the young today, someone shouted, they were discussing the young with all the bluster of the old, and then at the seventh hole, a man in the middle of his description, thank you, no ice, where was I? just imagine, he has still to let me have that preface, they were all talking at once: but in the little circle near my chair Anselmi was explaining one or two recipes of his success: go along with your readers, flatter their prejudices, if your hero is a poet, make him a hungry one, if he is a truly heroic hero, kill him off, if he is a rich man, show him as unhappy, things like that do not worry people, the secret lies in not robbing them of their illusions, but in that case, a voice objected, nothing will ever change, O you intellectuals, you always have that word on the tip of your tongue, but tell me this, when all is said and done, what is there to change? we should have learnt by this time that men do not change, come and see my Chagall, Francesca invited, Ric brought it from

Paris for me, could you wait just a moment, I answered, I did not want to miss the end of the lesson, all the more so because Anselmi was giving me a look that said we understand one another and this left me strangely uneasy, it disturbed me to find he was much more intelligent than I had imagined, and he must have considered me a phoney like himself, because at one point he winked at me, I thought the sweets would make me sick, how are you getting on with your novel? Ric asked point-blank, strange that no one thought of drinking a toast to the anniversary which had brought us all together, but you can't be going already, Francesca protested, come and see my Chagall, I felt my mouth cloying, perhaps because Ric keeps silver-framed photographs of her and the children propped up on his desk, and when he goes on his trips, sleeps with his secretary, perhaps that is why no one has raised his glass, I heard Anselmi's voice from the middle of his little audience, you just pave the streets with rubber and that will put a stop to revolution, and his hearers chorused in amusement, perhaps that is why everyone says: must see you again, must see you soon, before disappearing into the nothingness of the lifts.

The song of the sparrows, too, has meaning: those insolent chirpings which suggest a remoteness not simply physical, the silence between them which we listen to, unbelievingly, still straining to hear. But they do not sing in winter, they keep to their nests, perched among the bare branches. So I must have dreamt. Or say that a deserter has come through the lines, pierced the misty curtain right to the rail of our balcony.

'I don't know, dearest, it could be true.'

Emilia's theory is that a writer is a sick man, and that it is to cure himself that he writes, to lay bare, as it were, the roots of his own ill, in the process of analysis.

She answers from the bathroom, in monosyllables, with the clock-hands showing ten to eight, the heaters all off, shivering as she finishes dressing, because it is dark outside, the column of vehicles presses on along the avenue to enter the city, surrounds the underground passages leading from the station, they are coming, they have already reached Viale Corsica, I hear shouts of alarm.

She opened the outside door of the flat, she pressed to summon the lift, then came back inside for a moment to throw me a kiss and the paper which Luigino lays on our doorstep every morning.

I knew I was going to please her: I leapt out of bed and took hold of the shutter pull.

'What's got into you?'

She gave me a distrustful look, as if she knew that I would get back into bed the moment the door closed behind her, or, worse still, that I would be going out to keep some clandestine appointment.

'I have a contract to honour: I'm going to finish that damned book.'

That brought a flash of agreement, she remarked that she would probably not be back for lunch, there were eggs in the fridge and fruit too, so I would not be disturbed, I was alone and in sole possession of the field, there were other things she wanted to say to me but through the gaping door swirled the cold of the stairs, see you tonight, she just had time to say, I hoisted the blind right up, made coffee; a dull glow had flooded the room.

Half an hour later I was there at the typewriter, to the cracking of the whip that Doctor Y flicked about my ankles. I had left my heroine at page forty-two. I have never felt strongly that I was born to write: one glimmer of sun and my dedication goes. But the day was one of the best and the weather ideal for letting yourself believe that what you are engaged in writing . . . places and situations, dialogue and characters, traced out by the typewriter's chatter, is more real than reality, and that futile by comparison are even the linking up of the two astronauts in space, the recapture of the prisoner, the speech to the House, all of them ephemeral stuff beside what my characters were getting ready to do, beings with more lust and determination in them than any of the physically alive.

I found them as I had left them: shackled in mid-gesture, stills that had been held during the run-through, it was Doctor Y who had wanted me to stop the turning wheels of the projector, so he could study, with ecstasy, those uncompleted actions, the fore-shadowing of a game which hinted endless possibilities, because eroticism itself comes down to suspense, psychological tension, the ambiguous suggestion, perfect ordering of the elements, I was fascinated as I discovered its laws, I prepared slides, then studied them through the microscope, I drew back in horror, I looked again and confirmed to my astonishment that they acted of their own accord, independently of anything that I willed, going through a spontaneous process of decay, triumphant leucocytes writhed there even before I had ascertained it, if anything, they infected me with their feverishness, I want to become expert at it, whispered my married woman, so do I, lips against the window-pane, and, outside, a landscape like this one, mist, smoking breath, dew which drips under the dresses, I want to become expert at it, she repeated, her voice heavy with all the seductiveness of the first person feminine, that's it, exclaimed Doctor Y, keep on like that, even pornography can become art, I know, we are only at the beginning of the treatment, I shall write something that no one has ever dared put down on paper, I will transcribe sensations harder to come by than the cold delights of the sensualist, not the fade-out that becomes close-up, focused and enlarged, an eye that devours, a mouth exploring un-tried recesses, the stare that flays the skin, but rather the pauses, the images that come before the acts them-selves, even the words that gush out, suddenly released into consciousness, I had written a good ten pages straight off, I read them over with the satisfaction you derive from work well done, murmuring over the dia-logue, trying to hit the right inflection, Ric would come away from this horrified, perhaps he would offer to buy the manuscript himself, just so that he could throw it on the fire, and Francesca would be really shaken, but how can a woman like that exist, she would say, and a married woman too? precisely, a respectable, married woman, that is where you can still hit them, I heard Edo's snigger of pleasure, almost a Marxist thesis, while I ate before the wide-open door of the refrigerator, and then, while I was making coffee, we dwelt on our destructive plans, we inserted fuses, we prepared time-bombs, serums, poisons for injecting so gently, we were like scientists whose laboratory had a hated name.

It was two in the afternoon and the street lamps

along the avenue were already lit, the Brandenburg concerto swelled through the room, full volume, now it was the characters, on the unfinished page, who summoned me, no longer dummies or submissive extras, but human beings who, in their demoniacal urge, were truer than any I had ever drawn, in fact I struggled to keep up with them, to foresee their reactions, we were in no man's land, we ventured along paths of no return, together with them I savoured the pleasure of corruption, and the spade went scrape on the stone, as it lifted the chilly earth from the spot where the Divine Marquis, de Sade, is laid, and out of the cavities, one after the other, like sewer rats, came the fetishes of Eros, macabre, sinister: anatomical tables like maps, the wax genitals found in booths at the fair, foetuses in spirit, watch yourself, he said, watch yourself now, and I went down, I descended into the pit with them, forgetting every other law, in a universe of sweetness alternating with fury, I heard—it was like falling drops—three quarters sounding from a pendulum clock, the record had stopped, the dusk thickened the blanket of fog, I wrote 62 at the top of a new page, twenty sheets that some one had dictated, at a fever pitch I had never known before, to my obedient fingers, at first there had been starts, brief tremors, then the terrifying prospect of a landslide in myself as I threw off every restraint exactly like my married woman, breaking every moral law with her, enjoying the fierce compulsion to crime with her, without warning I felt the hot rush of an injection in my veins, something approached that was taking shape as a cloud, an overpowering smell, other faces urged, Denyse, Anselmi, Luigino the porter with his gap-toothed smile, or Ambro, the great critic, completely absorbed by those shattering pages, made notes, the typewriter no longer rapped, I read what I had written from the first word to the last, and they went through and, with infinite patience, went through again the selfsame gestures, the exact same obscenities, submissively they repeated unspeakable things, but I was the one to blush for them, I want to become, the woman repeated, she stripped naked and she dressed again, I dared not look her in the face, she sprawled back over the seat with the abandon of Miriam herself, even Doctor Y fell silent, I could just hear his breathing at my shoulder, he helped me to move the mirrors in silence, he loosened a fastening, then pressed it tight again, I want to become better at it than a prostitute, and suddenly she was no longer the one who was talking, erased by an impulse that was no longer hers, that came from me alone, the door opened, someone had come in, Emilia stared at me: I was holding Miriam, still drenched, in my arms.

The avenue that leads there begins at Stonehenge, in a landscape, already observed, of monolith, dolmen, menhir, it begins at Arles in the avenue to Aliscamps, passes right through the gateway of Porta Volta, as I was making ready to do myself.

I said to Emilia: the main avenue begins here. I had had to exert myself to convince her that there is nothing depressing about it, this is a sight they show tourists, ferrying them here in special buses for that very purpose, and lots of people come, like us, on Sunday, from the country places round about, and I hold her hand as our feet go crunch on the gravel of the central area, we go forward unhurriedly as if we were visiting an exhibition.

Every so often I glanced sidelong at her to see if her features expressed some reaction to our progress among the tombs, our stately pacing, unconcerned as royalty passing along the guard of honour at the airport, and I seemed to have carried out this inspection of stone angels at some previous moment in time, we walked on without confiding our impressions, just keeping in touch by a tightening of the fingers, a light pressure that conveyed understanding as we stood before a more magnificent, more sinister-looking dug-out.

'What a horror,' she sighed, as we sat ourselves on a low wall.

A cigarette returned us to the number of the living, her gloves laid on a shining block of black marble, no distance from the portrait, on an oval medallion, of a widowed lady of the Casiraghis, our breath steamed in the cold air, we were hidden, like tomb-breakers, behind an enormous yew tree, the leaden horizon gave us a new sense of space so that our steps led into another dimension.

'Ric asked me if we would like to go to Aosta with him,' Emilia said aloud. 'We could always arrange it.'

Gusts of wind flattened the jet from a little fountain, bent the willows until they brushed iron reliefs, little features copied from Egyptian tombs, feather-fans cut in porphyry, I detected a growing threat in the silence. Emilia raised an arm to gesture at it all, the action said what sense does all this have, but the words were not spoken, and I could not find them for her — to express the crushing sensation that comes from these reminders that we have done our duty by them, as if the dead were responsible for failings unknown to us, as if it were a virtue in us to be able to look on their memorials with calm indifference, on the names of famous houses humbled by the mist.

I wanted to say to her when we are there, we too will have circled back to nature at last, the trembling of a blade of grass, in the earthworm's coil, in the magnificence of the pine, facing an infinite which the high wall along Via Cenesio vainly strives to circumscribe.

'My feet are like blocks of ice,' said Emilia.

We rose up to the insistent call of a chaffinch, but I knew I would come back, on my own, to repeat this journey in the perfectly historic twentieth century, to reach those shores, a discovery you can make in a sonata for cello, oboe, and celesta: a still world which lets fall its drops, where I and all the others in the story dance in slow time.

An old woman went stooping from one headstone to another, furtively: unbelievable, said Emilia, they rob the flowers from the graves.

I must talk to you, I said to her as soon as we got into the car. But the dashing rain that streamed on my windscreen, from beginning to end of the motorway, made me watch how I drove, I kept my eyes on the red tail-lights of Ambro's big Ford going on ahead of us.

It was Emilia who had arranged this, the invitation had come to her — nothing said to me — at the office, to spend a week-end at their house on the Riviera. They were a strange couple, Ambro and Josephine. They would vanish for months at a time, then invite you to dinner at half an hour's notice. They had just come back from Gloucestershire, where they went for Christmas every year with the boys, staying with Josephine's parents. At the upper end of the Riviera rose their own house, one of those old villas, all turrets, set out on a cliff, that Josephine's forebears had built at the turn of the century, and later had walled in like an impregnable fortress. It was almost invisible, too, because of the greenery which, at this point of the coast, goes down, unbroken still, to meet the sea.

The glow burning between the slats woke me before Emilia herself, but she was the one who rose and ran over to throw the shutters wide; from the bed it looked as if that great blank of light had swallowed her up for a moment.

'Come and see.'

I threw my coat over my shoulders and looked out with her: the Tigullio coast came right into the room, the day was glorious as days in winter are here, you could see the bed of the sea, the veining of the different currents, the lazy slapping of wave on rock reached us and the fragrance of thyme, a wonderful morning, said Jo, when we were all gathered round the table for breakfast.

'How did you sleep?' she asked, pouring tea.

She looked even more fragile than usual, her eyes had the dark rings about them that come from drinking, or quarrelling, far into the night. There was damp in the walls, and we felt it entering our bones, but the curtains at the french windows already swelled out to the sunshine, a strip of light grew over the floor, the smell of bacon and eggs from the kitchen roused us.

'You see,' a radiant Emilia declared. 'We were right to come.'

I would have been glad if we could have clarified, she and I, just what it was that we had left behind us for a couple of days. Not the moment for such a conversation when Ambro was pouring grapefruit juice for everyone, we ate gaily, overwhelmed by all that light which still came on, but hunched up with cold, too, like the survivors picked up from a cruise disaster. As we ate, we watched the sea, or rather the line of sea and sky, all our gazes converging on one point, we talked about nothing in particular, spoons tinkled in cups, wonderful, Josephine kept repeating, with a catch like fear in her voice, only Ambro took his eyes off the scene through the window to glance at Emilia or pour himself more tea, pass toast, seemingly reluctant to join the rest of us in contemplation.

'Once, on a day like this, I and Jo, you remember that time in the boat?'

She swung round.

'Please — have you nothing else to regale us with?'

'Well now,' he laughed, 'we had rowed as far as the point there . . .'

'I told you to stop!'

Emilia rose up from table, I followed her example, luckily we had finished eating, I asked Ambro to show me his library, we were all on our feet now, and all embarrassed, the boys were playing in the garden, Josephine put on her sun-glasses, on that sweet face of hers the lips were drawn thin as a knife, she warned the boys to keep away from the water, Ambro packed tobacco into his pipe, thumbed it firm, we sprawled back on the sun-chairs, breathing our deepest, con- valescents from a disease which only Ambro seemed

69

immune to, massive as he was, a physical presence to reassure anyone.

'You were saying that, in your library . . .' I resumed.

'O don't talk shop,' broke in Josephine, 'not on a day like this.'

It was agreed that we would play a doubles at tennis, I and Ambro against the ladies, that we would then go for a walk to the nearby village, have lunch in a restaurant that they knew, and then a nap, and then an afternoon game of bridge, or a trip in the speedboat, yes, yes, shouted the boys, let's go out in the boat, Ambro sucked at his pipe in little draws, who asked for your opinion? challenged Josephine, run along and play with Miss Ann, a long and easy interval followed, the sea made clear lagoons of the little inlets below us, there was something we should have said, and which no one voiced, all of us being overcome by the view.

'Let's go down to the shore,' suggested Ambro.

He rose and offered his hand to Emilia, we had no choice but to follow him, a path slopes down steeply through the pine wood, you have to watch where you put your feet, the hand-rail is rotten, the ground, treacherous because of all the pine needles, I had to help Jo to steady herself at a couple of gaps. She was nervous as if fearing to be left behind.

Easy, I said to her, take your time. It was only too clear she was pursuing something, Ambro and Emilia had already begun on their way across the rocks and now went forward, by leaps, towards a great mass. Emilia stood motionless, legs apart, her feet braced on two little spurs, her scarf fluttered in the breeze, from behind Ambro steadied her, his hands at her waist, in another few seconds they would have flown off towards the sea, perhaps we would never have seen them again, so said Josephine's eyes, it was almost touching to see how uncertain she was in her beauty.

She suddenly stopped and said: 'Have you ever been unfaithful to Emilia?'

'No, why?'

She shrugged, grimaced, carried on right to the rock-mass, with her confidence restored, Ambro pointed out the holds to us, we hoisted ourselves up beside them, on a rugged face, sat as best we could. Once there, we took the freshness of the air in greedily, the quiet rocking of the waters, the salt tang that rises in gusts from the reef.

Our hands showed larger in the sun; I have always been afraid of this violent beauty that obliterates, this all-mightiness so apparent that it seems an invention, life itself becomes deception, as if . . . I don't under-stand, put in Jo, what do you mean?

As if death were truer, I thought, much more acceptable, less inhuman.

A stain, a clot that is still taking shape, I felt it growing and threatening us, just where the green of sea shone most intense, how could I be the only one to notice or perhaps the others ignored it, chased it away with a sweep of the hand as you brush off a fly, I like that tobacco, said Emilia, sniffing Ambro's way, they were headed for the offing, people waved from the coast, but, naturally, I wanted to explain to her, the professor may wear old shoes, but his tobacco is sent direct from Dunhill's of London, in fact I was on the point of saying it when the train burst out of the mountain side.

No one spoke then, each one of us being elsewhere.

The logs in the grate burnt without giving off heat. Through the open door I made out a line of rooms receding into the half-light, we were sitting in a ring around the fire, one enormous rug over all our knees, and the record was really something out of the ordinary, treble voices, perhaps from a choir school, singing and descanting God save the Queen, the music under that high ceiling, with the evening solitude upon us, made the crowning event of our day.

'Are you tired?' asked Jo.

Ambro and the boys had vainly tinkered with the outboard motor, the speedboat would not move. We had played tennis in the afternoon, as always, Emilia was striking them well, but Ambro's play was disastrous, he fluffed the easiest balls, so the ladies had beaten us in record time, at the pastry shop their famous cake was finished, we had to come back just after sundown, chilled to the bone, with a bag full of cans and two expensive woollen suits that Josephine had bought to give herself heart.

'Listen to this passage.'

Legs spread wide, Ambro beat time with his left foot. I was grateful to him for not discussing books.

'It's lovely here,' Emilia thought out loud.

'You should come more often,' Jo rejoined.

She forgot that, immediately previous to this, they had let a whole year go by without looking us up. And then Ambro cannot forgive me for having written, among my other productions, a book that has met with some success. His idea of literature is so aristocratic that he expects the writer to go through life misunderstood by his contemporaries, and, consequently, poor. This unyielding stance of his comes from his having married, along with Jo, enough wealth to merit the name of freedom from need.

'But this man here,' Ambro abruptly began, turning to Emilia, 'this man who's not saying anything, what is he writing at the moment?'

Emilia shot me an anxious glance.

'I *am* writing,' I answered. 'An unusual book, you'll see.'

'How far on are you?'

I explained that I was just at the beginning, I found it hard to talk about it, in any case, Ambro would not want to hear the plot, but if I managed to turn this story for men only into something worthwhile, I would give him the manuscript to read.

'You have to watch yourself,' he said with a paternal air, 'you make too many concessions in your books.'

My second novel he had reviewed enthusiastically in a serious magazine for language studies, and our friendship dated from then. I was in his debt for that proof of faith in me, not to mention the great influence he exercised, with his prestige, on a whole school of critics.

'Shall we play bridge?' suggested Jo.

The boys looked in at the door to say goodnight, the fire in the grate dwindled, the ice had melted in the glasses, I felt a longing for bed myself, but Emilia did not seem to notice.

When she joined me there, I was leafing through a book I had picked up in the library, it was almost midnight, the sheets were like ice, she snuggled up to me for warmth.

'A fascinating man, isn't he?'

Emilia never falls into that sort of trap: this time she readily agreed, but at once added that they were both charming.

I put the light out, we embraced in the gloom. The sea had risen, we heard its majestic breathing on the rocks, and that bed, which we were not used to, infected us with strange excitement, as always happens, let's cut our visit short, I said to her, and go tomorrow, it'll be better to cut our visit short, the figure of Ambro bulked enormous in that room, something was going wrong between him and Jo, but we could do nothing for them, we could do little enough for ourselves, I shall finish that book and then . . . I did not dare confess even to Emilia what I had vaguely sensed for a while now, we lay unmoving in one another's arms, winning back an intimacy that the day seemed to have undone, and then I'll begin something I don't know quite what yet, Emilia's hand tightened on mine, and it was at that moment that a shriek was heard, barely muffled by the thick walls, and then Jo's voice as she burst out sobbing, we held our breath as we listened, then silence wrapped us round again, we shouldn't have come, murmured Emilia, I saw her hit the ball clean and hard from the other side of the net, try and sleep, I said to her, and then her scarf fluttered back as she tried to cross rocks and water, keep that character, the married woman, for your heroine, Doctor Y himself had arrived, I felt myself fissured into a thousand trickles, without any sure centre, for the moment, beyond Emilia's bosom, I know that I thought: I must be stricter in my work, Ambro is right, I was grateful to him, after all, for the severity of his judgement, but I could not help him what with Jo still weeping, and if Emilia goes on beating the air with her racket, and through the closed window of his limousine Ric is saying something to me that I do not catch, I heard horns sounding from cars that waited in lines, I wanted

74

to tell them it will all pass soon, and it was no longer Jo weeping like that but my mother, as she stood in silence, before the refrigerator's open door.

All we could do was cling to one another in the dark. Away from here, some one was awaiting us, expecting us for an appointment of a kind, sure we would come.

There is something indecent in the way She stands above us, unseen; leaning over, as we do ourselves when we observe, from a balcony, the man who lives below. Indecent, that very situation which lets us watch him move and speak without ever suspecting. Because of the way we could hit him just as we pleased, choosing the moment and no warning given. So it is true, I was free to conclude, that all our striving and running about and inventing excuses to be somewhere else or with people is only to get away from Her, from the question She puts in our solitary moments. And if Ric shrugs the whole problem off and Emilia would never admit that it exists, this must still be what drives them in their daily bustling. Because you see, dearest, learning to be alone is already not to fear Her, growing accustomed to what we shall become. Listen to you, she declares, you've even turned prophet.

I know her answers. I said to her: damaged cells and fluids so tainted that the earth itself rejects them. Amazing, she smiles, why don't you run a column in the newspapers for readers' problems?

And yet I could reconstruct Her very features; give Her a face and a voice. If I attempt a picture of Her, She has the severe and slightly preoccupied air of some one who, from a distance, calls their dog to heel, and, in fact, the loop of a dog-lead hangs from one of Her hands, Her lips are already puckered to emit a sharp whistle.

It had snowed in the night. No plane has risen up this morning. I shaved carefully, this untainted whiteness will not last long, and then we should call Her by Her name, as the poets do, not be afraid to pronounce it, as they are in the very places where She is expected, hospitals and the firing-line.

I said Her name out loud, several times over, stressing it familiarly, as I sat before my typewriter. Everything that makes sense: to organize the materials given, will sound meaningless, the passion for art howled down, and the habitual regard for the classics as well, the manuscripts, too, which Emilia keeps shut in a case, in the attic, destined for posterity. Contrariwise great humility will be needed at the moment when this outward wrapping is given back, after our use of it, although today the snow seems to bring relief even to the corpses of the motor-cars down in the breaker's yard, docile monsters that slumber inside their enclosure.

I slipped on my overcoat and went out on the balcony: the air smelt of paraffin, the fumes had settled at roof-level under an oppressive sky, a few snow flakes were straying by still, the whiteness of them cleansed the eyes, washing away the dregs of a sleepness night, the phantom of Edo seated on a kind of little throne, like a sphinx, because he was moving his lips imperceptibly, in fact, I could not catch the words which came through a veil of dust, there were draperies, worn-out embroideries, the smell clothes have when you open a box in the attic, the stuff of childhood, according to Emilia, seeing that in dreams one is always subjected to a backsliding in time, I was in the middle of an obscure event which now, in the common daylight, kept its enigmatic character, if anything multiplied false leads, paths, countryside, gardens completely paved over, the earth and the stones everywhere wiped out by a flow of ashphalt, and Edo's voice repeats the invitation, obliquely urging to something I could not see but which must be there, within arm's reach, perhaps within the bounded waste of Linate, or in the smoke from the city's Shambles which fouls the air of this district, but the most extraordinary thing of all was to see my life, in the end, as a laughable episode, Emilia, I will tell her, I'm acquiring the sense of the precarious, you're wonderful, she smiled, peeling off her gloves, what next?

'Nothing: I just wanted to know how you were. If you'd heard from the lawyer, about your pension.'

Alarmed by this sudden interest, she answers. As she is reassuring me, she sounds almost offended. The training she gave me in reticence has always made me avoid pretty circumlocutions. At the moment I have to watch and not worry her, say, about the condition of her arteries.

'Why, do I look ill?'

'Go on,' I laugh, 'make me a coffee.'

Half-way along the corridor she halts, opens the door of what was my room: slippers at the bedside, someone else's jacket over the back of the chair, two bulky cases on top of the wardrobe.

'I've found a lodger. A young man, you know, the respectable sort.'

She shuts the door carefully, you would think it was no longer our house, and she cannot guess how humiliated I feel to see her reduced to letting rooms.

At the kitchen table there is already Signora Bernotti, one of those good women who forget their own worries in those of other people, and she is embarrassed as she greets me, in her worn, old dressing-gown, she rises up immediately to leave, she says she saw me once, I was talking on television, or in a newsreel at the cinema, she cannot remember which.

'When was that?' my mother asks. 'He never tells me anything about his work.'

I hear her voice rise and fall, the familiar rasping as she clears her throat, her wasted hands fitting the percolator together, and the man was saying: best of all is the Swedish black, you can have the slab cut to the exact size, six hundred thousand, that includes the actual siting and the inscription, if you want something cheaper there is always Val Camonica porphyry.

'Here,' said my mother, 'here's the beautiful outcome of it all.'

A sheaf of objections, official decisions, appeals copies of stamped testimonies, and at the end the people in Rome know nothing about it, perhaps the office that deals with these claims has lost the original document, the lawyer says if some one were to go to Rome in person . . .

'Let's hope for the best: your brother says he'll go, at the end of the month, with all the work he has to do, but he's the one who'll go.'

On the marble top of the kitchen table, her newspaper lies, folded back at the 'In Memoriam' notices which she and Signora Bernotti have been working through together, a daily inspection, roll-call, and the

78

one named takes a step forward, reading this consoles her with the thought that she has outlived some who were considered healthier, of better stock, that she will outlast them by a few years more.

'I must go,' Signora Bernotti finally decided.

Left to our silence we drank the coffee down, then my mother asked me if I would like a chocolate from the box I brought: it is still unopened.

'No, thanks.'

There is something ultimately irritating in this fixed rite, the rehearsing of all the good and bad our relatives have done, of her grandchildrens' surprising progress, the interest I have to show until the question is blurted out that she has been dying to ask for ages.

'And what about your father?'

'I don't know, I believe he's quite well.'

'I can see that he's going to be the hero in the end.'

I am well aware that I have disappointed her. Brought up to her unbending ways, I have come, myself, to accept compromise, to forgive my father for never having loved her.

'Look at this now,' she goes on. 'Nothing surprises me any more.'

They are erecting a building right in front of her windows, so that the little piece of sky she could turn to has become a crosswork of scaffolding, the house is even darker, strangled by its furniture, the setting for a middle-class comedy, where she goes about warily, starting at every ring on the phone, as she did in the old days, her hair gathered in a net.

'I'm not even any good at this now,' she says, waving to the unfinished crossword. 'The doctor says it's the pressure. When I get up in the morning, my legs almost give under me.'

My silence seems to confirm the desperate state she clings to. I ask myself what I could do to hearten her a little, something my brother manages much better, what with his family, his regular job, a handful of certainties, things my mother has succeeded in imbuing him with.

'O yes, my dear,' she says in the end, teeth clenched, arms tightening over her breast.

The odour of spirit, melted candles, the whirring of the ventilator fan, the deathly smell of roses hovered in that room, around her, and I could not let her know because my courage failed me. I could do nothing more than lay out the monthly sum on the exact same corner of the sideboard, as she turned away, as always, not to see.

Then say to her: 'It's cold here. You should buy a heater.'

My experience of life measures eighteen centimetres across: four novels, two of them bound in cloth, on the third shelf of my bookcase, and the dust that already works to turn them yellow, words which may grow with a little luck, and a lot of concentration, to twenty-three or twenty-four centimetres. But the hope of salvation that I put in them, in the glad beginning, fades more every day. Every time I have written a work, something has been left out, often the only thing I really felt urged to tell.

It was only now when I was engaged in faithfully transcribing the real, for Doctor Y's readers, that I could believe I was performing an act, a necessary crime, that I finally grasped a shred of truth in my hand, and the sense of fulfilment this gave me was so strong that I did not want to leave the desk when the door-bell rang.

'Come in,' I commanded, still striking the type-writer keys, and I had to repeat the invitation before a white figure broke from the hallway with an 'excuse me', the girl wore a dressing-gown that went down to her feet, she saw me in the ring of light from the desk, she halted in embarrassment.

'Is this yours? It fell down on my balcony two days ago . . .'

As a matter of fact, we had missed our bath-mat, perhaps I was the one who had hung it over the balcony rail, and so: don't mention it, said the girl, it's nothing, if anything I should beg your pardon for bursting in, she must have just got up, she had a curly head, a tired child's face, an expensive dressing-gown, because I live right below, she added, she had a Southern accent, I thought someone would have come for it, but since I am never in, I decided: fine, I put in, it was good of you, she looked all round the room, she asked: Are you the one who is always putting on church music?

Her manner suggested she did not want to go away at once, I invited her to sit down for a moment, no thanks, I must run, she said, settling herself on the edge of the bed, and then every so often I hear your typewriter rattling on, she had a strange way of speaking, in bursts, but then, I pointed out, you work at home yourself? excuse me, she said, I haven't even introduced myself, my name is Mary, but what sort of books do you write? her simplicity was unaffected, I heard from Signor Luigino down in the hall that there was a writer living above me, myself, I never have time to read books, an edge of her dressing-gown fell away, she had perfect legs, I wondered what she would have thought of what I was writing that very moment, perhaps at another time the situation would have excited me, but I wanted to dash off another three or four pages before lunch, I rose up and noticed that she was quite small, her eyes, still outlined with make-up from the night before, because being a shop assistant, she was explaining, I have this morning off, we moved slowly towards the door, it was very kind of you, miss, I was struck by her perfume, what a fashionable lady would use, assistant in a beauty parlour, she smiled, wickedly, excuse me for taking up your time, and at that point the lift stopped at our floor, the gate clacked open and Emilia stared at us as we stood motionless in the doorway, unfocused stupor in her gaze.

'Look at this, the bath-mat . . .'

Life might gain if we could carry over to it the easy naturalness with which, in dreams, we accept the most unacceptable situations. I am fascinated by the way that the personages there, having no moral life at all, are limited to pure gesture.

But, instead, Emilia passed between us, barely returning the girl's words of greeting, threw her handbag on the bed, pulled off her gloves and dropped them in the exact place where Miss Mary had been sitting a moment earlier: her look betrayed hurt, it said, is this how you work?

'She stays in the flat below, have you ever seen her?'

'No,' she answers, backing the words with a little forced smile, when she does that, she is inimitable, I want to crush her in my arms.

'Please,' she says, breaking free.

Now she has laid the table, out of the refrigerator comes our meal of cans, we eat in silence, she refuses to tell me anything about her morning at the Centre, you're being ridiculous, I was forced to say to her, what ever have you imagined?

She slips her shoes off to lie down for a short rest, the radio emits the pips for two o'clock, dance music takes over, Emilia had begun to look through the paper but with a gaze that suggested that she was thinking: this house is too small for two people, the debris of the meal on the table in our kitchen alcove, a still life of plates and bottles, we, too, were about to be swallowed up by the advancing city, by the clanging gong of the steel tubes tipped in one mass from a lorry's back, to crowd the edge of the new building site.

'Emilia,' I called.

I went up to her, without lifting her eyes she made a place beside her, I sat on the edge of the bed near to her legs, I watched her as she read with absorbed detachment, and her aloofness was exciting since I felt certain she would repulse me, and, sure enough, she pushed my hand away, I invite you to dinner tonight, we could do a show, or there is the private view of that exhibition, I'll pick you up at the office, we'll have a little drink in town, I was glad she left me this much terrain to be aggressive in, my hand closing on her knee, but it was only too clear that we were running away from something, an involuntary sigh broke from her, then another which my lips smothered.

There are actions which memory stores as unique although they have been repeated times without number: the way Emilia keeps her legs, when she is lying on her side in that attic room at Lucerne, her shoes on the bed-mat, and the wet breath of the downpour came in at the window, the ring of mountains had vanished, the Pilatus itself lost in cloud, from the bed I saw the two slate domes of the Catholic church and the glistening copper balls atop them, people were sheltering under the roofed walk of the wooden bridge, a solemn tolling of bells across from the Volksbank, one flaunting swan has stayed behind to attempt the current of the Reuss, the manes of the chestnut trees lining the river-bank stir fresh with rain, how did it go? I asked her from the bed, the professor has refused to budge from Vienna this year, she had answered as she took off her shoes, the sky was breaking clear above the tiles of the Hôtel du Pont, from the lake the hoarse siren hoot of a steamer came through to us.

'Your shoes,' I said, 'at Lucerne.'

There was a spider lying in wait on the moulded cornice of the ceiling, a palm's width off our vertical, outside, the flanks of the towers had been lit up, the steeples, the enormous clocks, and the lamps along the bridge, and the black waters of the Reuss, lit with glimmers, domes and garrets, battlements, pinnacles, belfries, window-boxes of geraniums, pennants fluttering along the streets fell silent with the night breeze, Emilia had dozed off, her back to me, I felt its contours entering my side, and the sweet peace of it I could never forget.

'Let me go, it's almost three.'

The spider had moved about six inches towards the window, Emilia moved her legs, the gusts crackled over the river, ruffling the smoothness of the flow, with one hand she mechanically stroked her shoulder, a long sigh, the orchestra has struck up at the bar below, we should have booked at the Raben or the

Federal, I had even noticed mosquito legs on the wall beside the bathroom mirror, we had risen up together and looked out, naked, upon the river's gloom: along the terraces of the restaurants the lamps seemed chapel lights.

A transparent theatre-curtain, a hanging veil opened for us alone. At this moment, I had thought, nothing could touch me, fierce chords in minor, solemn horns echoed inside, and out, of that room sunk in night, unbelieving we had made love again, bent over her body I distinguished the last flashes that struck at us from the rifts in the clouds, then my cheek against her ear, my breath on her neck, I had imagined I had given Her the slip again, outdistancing Her shadow.

Now She had come back to settle herself patiently, no great way from our pillow, waiting at the threshold with her unchastened gioconda smile.

'I need another month. I can't make it, for the dead-line we fixed—I'm sorry.'

Doctor Y took off his spectacles, carefully polished the lenses, held them to the light as he squinted through, finally said: 'Will you have a whisky?'

From a compartment in his desk emerged bottle and glasses, at that moment his secretary's voice rasped through the intercom, try and stop him, answered Doctor Y, probably the police have come into it, I thought, so that's the problem solved fair and square, yet the efficiency of this publisher's office, the Swedish furniture, the deodorant in the air, the thick, blue carpet, the mock-up of covers displayed on a large board behind the boss's head served to reassure me.

'Now,' he began after his first sip, 'about the book –
we've read all that first part that you sent us.'

I hung on his words like a novice.

'My view is: the first part, fine. But there's a factor
we don't see eye to eye about.'

He opened the typescript, thumbed it through casu-
ally, but it was obvious that he was looking for one
special place which he could no longer find.

'This style you have, at times it is too . . .'

He searched for the epithet, his hands came to the
rescue, they described a vague round on the air.

'Too . . . cloudy-like, say.'

'Nebulous,' I said.

'Perfect. But what you really have to do is to hit
the reader,' and he raised his fist threateningly, 'hit
him with the shattering details of sex . . .'

Why do I not rise up? I wondered. One of the models
on the covers looked like Jo. It is a tough profession,
this one, not learnt in a day, and Doctor Y was wonderfully patient as he instructed me, because my text as
it stands would never be translated in Copenhagen,
what had all that yarn about her being corrupted for
love of a man to do with it, a modern writer like you,
warned Doctor Y, has to worry about foreign editions,
forget the love business; it is strange how people
depict love as something miserable and allow death
greatness, not noticing the over-simplicity of the
clinical description, the voice of the surgeon who
demonstrates how the fragment, passing through
the left occipital region, travelled right on, a very
interesting case, to the top of the spinal cord, and
from there to the right hemisphere, but the resemblance
to Jo was really disturbing, that angel gaze above the
nipples clasped between parted fingers, I was dis-

tracted, too, by a voice blaring through a megaphone down in the street, a march of strikers with placards and banners which was going forward on Corso Europa.

'I trust I've been clear alright?'

'Perfectly clear.'

He had marked some passages in red, as needing to be rewritten. I had come along to suggest to him that perhaps there was a way of writing the story that I would find less debasing, and that would bring him even more prestige, but a chorus of loud whistles from the marchers in the street and the megaphone voice's appeal to the people stopped me, workers! they shouted, workers! nothing else was intelligible but it was evident that Doctor Y was right when I had no objections to make, on the contrary I rose up, took back my typescript, shook his hand.

'My view is: the first part, fine. Go on like that, right to the end.'

So you get that kind of see-sawing of the road as it winds, and beyond the last curve the outline of the menhir show, erect above the green plain, the unbelievable stones of the Celts enclosed by barbed wire: I was paying another visit to the very place I had explored a few days earlier with Emilia, but this time I did not have to share even one of my thoughts. I have never learnt any other style of going walks, even if Stonehenge is only one little plot of this ample cemetery, going on at the pace that leaves at my back the skyscrapers of that little Manhattan, industry's towers competing against the glass and steel of the public services, perhaps it will be here, the experts on the deterrent suggest, that the potential of the initial strike will fall, in the event of massive retaliation or simply of flexible response: here where dialect is erased, a few tiles surviving the bulldozers where there was once the network of districts, alleys, railings, the ineffable in art, as Ric calls it when he lets himself go.

'We'll come on Sunday, without fail,' I had had to promise him.

The conifers bordering a sky of too intense a blue, sunlight cutting across the bunches of chrysanthemums, and cold that was keen enough to crack the varnish upon the votive lamps: my troubled wandering ran the danger of turning into a lucky archaeological outing. I would have preferred it if it had rained, to see water pouring over the marble slabs, the dripping from the ironwork, a glitter of metal through the mist, and I chose a bench between ancient pines, cobwebs quivered against the light, trying to see if the mind can still be 'fired to excelling things', but actually distracted by the rumbling of the traffic at Porta Volta, and all the time, with a twig, I traced undecypherable signs in the fresh earth of an exhumation.

Instinct which we trust so little should guide our hand: the stick drew segments, a circumference broken into arcs, signs that looked all mixed together, initials in capitals, triangles, hypoteneuses, the E of Emilia, shorthand of a dead language, and then symbols that were immediately censored by good taste, an unexpected reminder of Miriam only half-drawn—a profanation, this, of the 'urns of the strong', not far from a granite base, a whole alphabet of uncertainties out of which came an S, that swept right back on itself, the curve of the earth-worm, a cluster of them which now, at last, I could make out as if that fresh earth were a pane of glass, the rotting universe that fights against the marble of Candoglia, the diorite, the funereal sheets of lead and zinc, steel partitions clammy with slugs, and my hand trembled as I scored the earth, I glimpsed, a few yards below, radiographs that were almost perfect, and myself become skeleton, like the view from a terraced garden over a valley, my flesh crept as I gazed on that void gaping unannounced, I do not remember how long I stayed there, I know only that a chord suddenly resounded, and then another, within those hollows; some one had sat themselves at the harpsichord, liquid notes were borne from those cavities, crypts, mausoleums, they massed together and broke apart again, how can it be, you thought, that we are mistaken about everything, startling harmonies, preludes and fugues were coursing in the earth's veins now, I tried to keep off the pity for myself which was about to assail me, and the twig hung down limp from my fingers, powerless to evoke new rites, overcome by the messages that came through to me more and more clearly.

I bent down till my ear was grazing the earth, and then, as the concerto was muted, I caught a trilling of little bells, the ticking of stop-watches, and lastly a siren howling from beyond the monuments to announce the end of the shift, and from the topmost pinnacles of the mausoleums sprang smoke of factory chimneys, the glories of Milanese industry in the sunset hour, and the gates closing with a harrowing shudder, on the bones of the great captains.

'That way for the exit,' the keeper called out to me.

Then other gates, but these only temporary, closed behind me.

'I heard them down there, you know? Working away.'

Emilia sniffs: she knows I am not simply joking. I have committed follies enough to reach my present posture—stretched out beside her, in the dark, as I talk, wide-eyed, on this bed that takes up most of the room.

'What then?' she asked, after a pause.

My right hand and her left lie clasped upon her abdomen, level with her iliac, sound its consistency, test the epithelium's texture, at times my finger-tips briefly reconnoitre no man's land, they advance right to the inward of her thigh, especially if our discussion comes to a point of tacit understanding, a satisfying answer.

'Then I thought: perhaps the prize is just that: nothingness.'

She nods, her lips pressed tight, the look she always has when analysis has only just begun and she is mentally noting facts.

'I've wanted to talk about it with you for a while now, long before today.'

That is, I wanted to discuss whether the punishment is not this, rather, that we drag our obsessions along with us, even after. Unable to free ourselves from vices and fears. Infecting other elements.

We float on silently for a quarter of a minute, the sea, dead calm.

Then Emilia asked: 'Your mother?'

'She comes into it. It's all terribly complex.'

Her comments are restrained, although she knows she is the only one who is free to elaborate on these things to the point of telling me unpleasant home truths. Don't lose heart, her hand says, and I have to choose my words for fear of passing on my bewilderment to her. It is strange that I never thought of this sooner.

'It's not so strange, really,' she answered.

If what we are discussing should come between us, our hands will draw back, we shall talk from two open tombs, and it is very interesting, this ability to comment on facts which touch the past and the present of us who have passed away, that is if you take lying out prostrate as a rough proof of decease.

'You find everything as it should be, Emilia.'

I propped up the pillow, sat up against it. Every so often the shutter slats quivered in the wind. This is the proof, she explained, of the decadent characteristics in your make-up, and she pronounced this with the professional manner that I cannot stand.

'I didn't ask you to solve my problem: I wanted to talk, that's all.'

We were coming down, and now, as our descent quickened with an unexpected current, we could make out once again a terrain we had flown over a thousand times.

'Sorry, I'm tired.'

She came and sought refuge under the wing of my arm, a lorry had entered the exit-lane, it slowed down, roaring all the while, like the first vehicle of a convoy, I had her hair on my shoulder and her face upon my chest, enough to reassure anyone, but I saw the lorry drivers, muffled up, at the wheel, each in his cabin, a dangerous suite for oboe and bassoons, Emilia, I said to her, don't go out tomorrow, the ground must be hard, no digging a grave in it, and there will be bodies lying unburied, stiff in their overcoats, laid out on the steps leading down to the tube, and the emptiness of

91

our discussion struck me so forcibly, and so elusive proved the question that I had wanted to put, and her body so real amid all these abstractions, that it ended as it always does.

Many things were to change from that night. But in the manner of real changes, without those involved, neither I nor Emilia, suspecting it.

Part Two

THE valley dipped down before us, a streak that was Highway Twenty-six cut straight across that blinding white, the clumps of firs on which the shadow of this Blanik glider printed itself, and under us, to the right, the flying club like a small-scale model, with its hangars and the grey ribbon of the runway.

'Now!' Ric's voice commanded.

I pulled the release: the cable shot free, sank gently through space, the glider slowed its flight, hovering.

'Look: the Gran Paradiso.'

'Where?'

'Down there, to the left.'

The air whistling by was the only sound to tell us we were alive in that silence, it made us raise our voices as we soared up the mountain pass, Ric had had little trouble in persuading me to come: the brilliancy of the sky, the snow carpeting the depths of the valley urged the experience on me.

'God!' I said, 'it's wonderful!'

The altimeter registered just over three thousand feet, our speed was fifty miles an hour, I looked back and caught sight of the launching harness just as it hit the ground. Ric had explained to me that if we were lucky enough to meet rising currents, we could stay up an hour.

'There's the Paradiso again!'

Bedazzled, I glanced. I wondered how I would get out of this kite in an emergency, immobilised as I was by buckles and webbing.

'Which is the first strap I should pull?'

I heard him snigger in amusement: no matter, it is the grip I had on my chest, nothing to be afraid of, you are clear in three seconds, only – do not lose your head, and the sun played flashes along the wing, set the snow ablaze, what about it, Ric returned to the attack, fantastic, eh? now we'll do a little stunting, do we really have to? I demurred, nothing to fear, keep relaxed, another glider wheeled some three hundred feet above us, it spiralled, it looped, I pointed it out at once to my pilot.

'I've seen him: it's that crank Vasini!'

We were headed for a mountain side, the steadiness with which Ric aimed at some mark there was unnerving, the pinnacles of the fir-trees loomed near, I breathed again when we veered just as the conifers came right up under us, I'm hunting for a current, Ric explained to me, but there's this blasted calm, now we were gliding again in mid-valley, his assurance was exhilarating, it gave me a sense of power, I'm picking up speed, he warned, prepare for a loop! the indicator jumped, a dive and we turned right over, the body dragged back by a giant hand and crushed right down into the cockpit.

'How did it go?'

I had to admit that the 'death-flip' was stupendous, but I had pins and needles in my fingers and my toes.

'Cold?'

I was almost frozen stiff, but a remnant of pride stopped me from saying it out, we were sweeping in large circles around one point, the nose pointing at the Bianco chain, then on to a rugged outcrop.

'Here, you take over!'

I began by trying the joy-stick, the fluid motion of

the rudder-bar, at my back Ric supervised, repeating orders, but it still terrified me to see the fir-clumps on the mountain sides come rushing up, easier! my instructor's voice broke in again, we flew low over a gully, in line astern from Vasini's glider, below us the ribbon of cars placidly unknotted, meanwhile there was something I should do from this height: warn them, put them on their guard, because they had not the least notion of how long they were to last, and suddenly I saw our glider smashed among the crowding trees, our two bodies lying on the quilt of snow, sunk down among moss and lichen, wreckage hanging from branches, and I dwelt lovingly on this image, of us stretched out on the marmot's crumbling trail, on those vertical tracks that the thaw would melt as it would melt our features, and I was amazed that I could accept this quite naturally, this possibility that would strike Ric as simply ridiculous, unprepared as he is for any such event, and my discovery filled me with joy, I felt a strange elation possessing me, now I was navigating carelessly, unmindful of my instructor's advice.

'Not like that, you're banking too steeply!'

I felt a sharp reaction from the rudder-bar, the glider righted itself. Only today do I see how you could give in to this powerful incitement, be led to play with Her, mock Her where she lies back in Her lair, provoke Her into emerging, while you are still whole in yourself, with sound nerves, muscles tensed strong, in the pure joy of the physical, present Her with a challenge, but for Ric all this is a matter of simple technique.

'Watch now, here's a current!'

Ric took over the controls again, the kite pointed

its muzzle way up high, the wave was rising, the joy-stick back on your chest, it made you exult a little to be borne up to the right height again by a natural force, and then come away from it in wide sweeps, going down towards the earth again, having seen the empyrean, while points of frost have begun to form on the plexiglass over the cockpit.

'Now we'll try a stall!'

Involuntarily I thrust my gloved hands out to catch hold of something, Ric guffawed in delight, he was like a boy trying a new trick on a grown-up, just then the glider slowed down until it was almost stationary, began to shudder violently, I saw the joy-stick go down before me and the nose pitch in a dive, into the void, a few seconds when the blood was drumming at my ears, my stomach left to take care of itself, and we had come out safely again, planing along smooth.

'My legs are absolutely numb, Ric!'

He himself must have been purple with cold, we carried out a last reconnaissance of the valley; a few minutes later the tail skid was sending up sparks from the runway's tarmac.

Emilia had come to fetch us with her car, she helped me out of the cockpit, she had followed all our evolutions through a pair of binoculars, there was not a trace of anxiety in her voice, we could have been getting down from a roundabout.

'How did your pupil perform?'

I was a block of ice but I could not hide my childish satisfaction from her. I would have been glad to go off with her alone now, recount the confused intimations I had had a few minutes earlier, tell her of the fear that inhabits the lives of the great: that a silly accident may cut off the greatness they have been marked out for, although Emilia maintains that great men have never existed, except for the ones produced by circumstances. Her ideal is a society made up of our friends multiplied several times over, a confederacy of equals. But what awaited us in the flying club restaurant was a table-full of Ric's pilot friends: I'll just slip this kit off, he said, and I'll be with you.

The table was laid with style, some little warmth from the sun behind the curtains, the snow outside the window, Emilia had to sit at the other end from me, Ric arrived in a knitted jacket, ordered his rare-done fillet and grapefruit juice, the atmosphere was that of an outing in the country, after lunch we'll run up to Saint Vicent, suggested Vasini, I've got some likely numbers for the roulette wheel, but conversation at once came back to flights, to the latest types of glider, and the competitions at Rieti next season.

'I met the Professor the other day.'

It was the name Ric reserved for Ambro, compounded of respect and irony.

'He is putting an anthology of prose-writers together.'

'That so?'

I found myself wondering why Ambro had not mentioned it, probably from a kind of shyness.

'It will give you a boost, when you come out with your new book.'

If there is one thing in Ric's vitality that irritates, it is his inability to cut loose from his work.

'I don't know, I'm still a lot behind.'

I would much sooner have asked him how he manages every time that he is hovering in air, not to consider the possibility of a sudden end, but he had turned away to explain to Emilia what diamonds are, a complicated sum of sporting achievements thanks to which Ric already possessed two diamonds, but the third, he was saying, would have to be won in France.

I wanted to know what the secret of not fearing Her is, but I did not mean the device employed by people like him, of putting the thought of Her away each time it arises, and I envied him that sureness which had been mine too, up to a short while before, and that I had now lost beyond recall. Certainly the day was of a kind to make these ideas of mine less acceptable than ever, and after our coffee we went out and sat in the sun, squatting on the restaurant steps, a gang of students crowded together for the photo to mark the occasion, at last I had Emilia by my side, her head resting on my windbreaker, her hair dishevelled by the piercing breeze, they had left off talking, in fact Ric had fallen asleep, sitting propped against a door-post.

'Come for a little walk,' Emilia suggested, turning up the collar of her fur coat.

We wandered off behind the hangars, the crust of the frozen snow refused to yield, we could have gone right on up the valley without tiring ourselves. The great roller-doors of the hangars were pushed wide, you could see the gliders lying with one wing-tip rested on the concrete, Ric's Blanik was still out in the open, dazzling in the sun, a flight now might have been more exhilarating with the wind that was rising, what did you say, asked Emilia, nary a word, in fact it was strange how everything I had felt up there was proving to be untranslatable; or, rather, the wish to translate it had left me, and Emilia did not seem anxious to know.

Once again, the view before our eyes overwhelmed us, as it had done that morning by the sea with Ambro and Jo: the mountain slopes around us, that massif, white as milk, against the enamelled sky, or perhaps it was the awareness of a serenity that it would be too hard to preserve, a privilege which, one way or another, we shall pay for, really, she would have said, you never let good enough alone, but even Emilia seemed content to be simply going forward, hand in hand, at random, over that stretch of snow, leaving behind her the shadow of the girderwork and her pitiable mental cases, as I, the shameless tale I was composing for the pleasure of Doctor Y and his readers.

'Let's go back,' I said.

Once again paradise lost was transmuted to resigned gladness.

Classical quality has no rules: it gets right inside, it makes an incision, it cuts and goes away. A scratch is left, an invisible wound, and the blood begins to flow, miraculously, because of that secret impulse. For years I have tried to see into the possible laws which govern it, to lay bare its essential nature: the remoteness, above all, of the voice, and then its incomparable timbre, its superb (and conscious) artistry. If I succeeded in raising my book to this level, I could even boast of having written it, and, who knows, sign it with my own name, show Ambro I was not making concessions, open new horizons of publishing for Doctor Y, silence Emilia's doubts about my future.

But the refuge of man is to invent theories to account

for his weaknesses as soon as they arise, to discover that they have an inevitability about them in the crazy scheme of existence.

When all is said and done, what lay beside the phone was a reminder that my insurance should be renewed, income-tax forms, and the bill, already overdue, for the telephone itself. And outside the rain.

The car would not start this morning Emilia said, as she came back in. Less than a hundred pages to do, I answered. Then the overture to the afternoon, the lamp lit beside my portable, water dashing on the balcony, the keys resume their striking. Literary creation goes forward by swirls of activity, blockages, sudden leaps. Having spent the morning reading the papers, I expected words forming up on my page to draw me after them, unaided, instead I was acting like the painter who tries out the colour loading his brush on the palette's edge, as I broke off to work out snatches of dialogue, descriptive background, the cast of a sentence, on odd scraps of paper. Technical considerations which I had thought I could ignore in the book for Doctor Y, but which were now inescapable if I was going to elevate its style and content.

Meanwhile I had to get back that rhythm again, the tension I had reached when I left off. It was obvious to me now that this was not to be done by simply describing the same kind of action over and over, mechanically (what you get in books of this kind and which makes them not unlike cookery manuals), but only by showing those actions as they are refracted by emotion, psychological tension, the consciousness of sinning, the awareness of what we call the forbidden. As it was, Doctor Y had put his finger on it at once: it is the process of corruption which fascinates. And then he had added: 'no limit at all.' This liberty was a trap: I had tried to avoid it by falling back on stylistic devices, but at our second meeting Doctor Y had put me on my guard against this: 'too nebulous,' and I had a visible reminder of that warning, in red pencil, on those pages in Part One.

I read the last five sheets over, then, going further back, ten more. They sounded as if they had been written by some one else, set down under the influence of a hallucinogene drug, no wonder they had made Emilia indignant, when to read them left me perturbed; I was discovering a side of my nature quite unknown to me, my ability to overstep every bound, shock all sense of decency, a potential of vileness in myself that I would never have suspected. He never tells me anything, about his work . . . My mother would refuse to understand. You are not well, Ric would gravely pronounce, you need a rest. Ambro would shrug, but eloquently. Josephine would dip into it, in secret. To everyone of them I could retort that all this was worth two million lire, two million for a couple of months work, to be perfectly honest, there was more to it than that: behind those paper figures, beyond the female character who spoke in the first person, throbbed the memory of a quite different experience: my story with Miriam, years earlier, how that had been.

More than an hour had gone. The first sheet of the day waited in the typewriter carriage. Out on the stairs a door slammed. Miriam was there before me, biting back her lower lip prettily, the unbearable rustle from her stockings.

'You've come,' I murmured.

The keys began tapping again, frenziedly. That vileness swept me along, gave me ten times the energy: on an afternoon like this, in the house where I had lived alone, I had spent empty hours waiting for her, starting each time the lift mounted up, straining to hear her step, but how did this ever happen? I kept saying to myself, a girl like another, who is twenty years younger than you, that's alright, I told her on the phone, it doesn't matter if you cannot manage today, I'll come for you tomorrow, because her fiancé had turned up in front of her house to see her, and as we are getting married in the spring, she said, he must not know about us, I'm really crazy, we shouldn't meet again, Miriam, I cried, I believe that you, I believe that I, you know, no other woman, I struggled to let her know what that lily of her body was, that unviolated flesh, how her breasts under the cheap sweater were torment to me the evenings she let herself be carried off in my car, straight from work.

'I'll do it,' she said gravely, 'you'll see, I'll do it.'

I unwrapped her middle, I saw a riot of lace where there is only a triangle of nylon, as soon as I could switch off and brake near the flyover, Miriam abandoned herself to my fondling, at this hour of the night the area around the petrol station is a dark clearing where no one will disturb you, we had halted by the pumps, with all lights off, come over here, I said to her, one kiss and already my hand was moulding her back, pressing those yielding muscles, that smooth fleshiness with restrained fury, I infected her with my impatience, then a breast that budded in the mirror, she lay back on the seat, legs wide, you'll have to come to my place, I kept saying, and she answered with her childish no, while my left hand explored her, just because no, she said again, giving a start, her weal showed in the light from the dashboard, a soft crinkle faintly traced, her legs stretched out on the car's thick mats, a prey made ready in the chromium glitter, her side, bared now, rubbed on the gear-lever knob, seemed to dare it to try and pierce her, and then why don't you love me, she said opening herself again, the limbs' shining outdid the red of the seat, led me on to a journey in the forest that was easily enough undertaken, the windows steamed with the heat inside, I felt myself sliding under her gaze, in the awareness that I would never know anything else like this, nothing else so intense that I wanted to shout aloud with it, and I did shout to her, uttering the word that had made her shiver the first time, that's what you are, I shouted, my mouth on her mouth, you are the only one, the true one, I cried aloud, grappled to her, and the driving mirror, tilted her way, transmitted an image of triumph, because you make me, she panted, breathing out words and sighs, broken sentences, the odour of her nakedness saturated that little space, enjoy this too much; and her hair, all loose, covered her mouth, stop, please: this will kill me, it is all you want, lying back on the head-rest, she exposed herself now without any shame, it's not true, it's you who are so great, who are too much for me, I began to rumple her again, the two of us shaken together by a delirium which at each new meeting caught us up and left us trembling with weakness.

'Are you happy?' she asked as she leant her forehead on mine. 'I've given up my boy friend, see?'

It was she, with her child's hands become motherly, who wiped the sweat from my face, each time I was amazed that the engine roared to life again, that the car moved off, that it was unaffected by all that sweetness.

You know, I had said to her, with my eyes closed, I almost always see fields, grass, streams — what do you? My heart had come back to its place, Miriam was pulling down her dress, her little breast was guarded again.

She stared out through the windscreen, the darkness was broken by oncoming lights, and I shall never forget the tone in which she said it: I see the day you'll leave me.

Living near an airport has its drawbacks, for example, you can take the noise of a Trident roaring off for the voice of God, especially towards nightfall, but it has the advantage, too, of keeping you in constant touch with the outer world.

Emilia can even recognize certain flights, like the 19.50 for Paris and London, can identify winking navigation lights for the last plane to Zurich.

'That's what it must be,' she asserted, glancing at her watch.

'Then you're going to be late for the film.'

Francesca had suggested they go to the cinema together, Ric has been in Madrid for two days now. The rain had stopped, but I could not face dressing to go out, I was going to wait for Emilia at the television set.

When the bell rang, I felt sure that she must have forgotten something: I was taken aback to find myself facing our shapely neighbour from the flat below.

'Please, could you come downstairs a minute?'

She was wearing a pullover, her hair was awry.

'I have a friend there, a man, he's taken ill . . .'

Her look was beseeching; genuinely so: please, she repeated, taking me by the hand, then as we went down the stairs together, she added: 'This has never happened to him before.'

The man lay motionless on the bed, a double bed as large as ours but pushed against the other wall, so that the room seemed of a different shape and size altogether. We went over to him in the discreet light from a lamp, his gaze did not seem to register me.

'I can't understand it,' said Mary. 'It all happened without warning, like a stroke.'

The wheezing, almost animal breathing of the man made him something alien in that room, beads of sweat glistened on his face, acting by instinct, I loosened his collar, we should have tried to revive him, do something but I was ignorant of what.

'We'll have to call a doctor.'

'O yes? And then what?'

The thought of having to explain it all worried her, perhaps, too, the prospect of trouble with the police.

'Listen, if he dies, it'll be a lot worse.'

He was a man of about fifty, burly, well dressed to judge from the jacket and shoes he had thrown into a corner of the room.

'When did this happen to him?'

'Ten minutes ago: I dressed and ran upstairs. I was hoping that you . . .'

He had moved his right arm meantime: slowly he placed the open palm on his chest, a faint rattling came from his throat.

'A brandy would do the trick,' said Mary.

The room smelt of a kind of soap, I glanced around: on a little table were laid out a tube of shaving cream, a freshly lathered brush, and a safety razor.

'Listen,' she called softly as she leant over him, 'listen, we're here beside you, you'll see that it's nothing really.'

He opened his mouth. Straining towards us, he tried to utter some words but they would not come. An expression of deep stupor came over his features, I lifted his wrist, to take his pulse, just to be doing something, his eyes, staring wide, questioned me, he must have taken me for a doctor and probably, in my place, Emilia would have been more helpful.

'What is it you feel?'

With his hand he touched his chest, pointed to his left arm: from the little I knew about it, he had suffered a heart attack, one which could dispatch him to the next world.

'Where's the phone?'

Mary let out a cry: let's wait, she begged, let's just try and see if he comes to, if a doctor arrives on the scene, they'll bring charges against me, I'm not from Milan, they'll send me away, she was on the point of bursting into tears.

'Look,' I insisted, 'this doctor is a friend, there won't be any consequences.'

I dialled his number, an answering service replied, I dictated the message and sat down to wait. The man had closed his eyes, his feeble breathing invaded the silence, his face was a heavy mask of pain in the muted light.

'Perhaps we should prop him up?'

I said it was better not to touch him until the doctor came.

'You were busy working, weren't you?' the girl said apologetically.

I was wondering how he had suffered a turn like that with his trousers still on, before he had even begun.

'Was he shaving?' I asked.

'Well,' she answered: then went on: 'Would you like a coffee?'

She did not want to give me details, but she would have to tell it all to the doctor.

'He's someone very . . . he's a gentleman,' she told me at last, speaking from the little kitchen. She ended by letting me know he was very fond of her, so much so that he drove over from Turin, every two months, all for her, and he had been doing that ever since they met the summer previous.

'At Turin?'

'No. A mutual acquaintance gave him my telephone number, because . . .'

Her voice dropped as she spoke, it took on the tone of someone who has been the victim of a confidence trick.

'That's all he wants to do. You understand now?'

I looked back at the table where the implements testified that the process had not been completed.

'He had just begun, when, all at once . . .'

Those feet so large in the socks, displaying their broad soles, imprinted themselves on the eye, as shapes already seen, a premonition of a sinister kind, with a shudder I imagined her naked posture when it had all happened, I felt like walking out, afraid of being involved in a sordid incident.

'How much sugar?' she said.

I fancied I could not detect his breathing any longer:

I rose up, the man opened his eyes for an instant, I bent over him to mop his brow with a face-cloth. Stretched out on that bed, the coverlet little crushed by his bulk, he seemed to be on a catafalque, I was struck by the insolence She has in intruding, Her outrageous self-assurance, the humiliations She inflicts on us before the final blow.

'Bear up,' I murmured, 'the doctor's coming.'

We had to wait another interminable hour, watching over the man as he lay in his terrified silence. Mary rose up every so often, to wipe his sweat away and comfort him with conventional phrases. At last the phone rang.

'I'll come down and open up for you,' I answered. 'Try and be quick.'

We sat down again, an alarm clock shrilled noisily from the kitchen, Mary had set it when the man arrived because often he falls asleep afterwards, in fact, at this moment he should be bowling along the motorway to Turin, but who knows how it happened, she concluded, I can't understand it at all.

'Are you expecting other visitors?'

She gave me an offended look; anyway, an evening like that, she quickly told me, brought her as much as she would make in a month as a shop assistant, because she had found a shop assistant's job when she first came to Milan, but then she earned too little, and so . . .

Her shamelessness disarms you, any words she utters sound a lie: the hardships she underwent in those early days, the talk of family, still there in her hometown, her father ill, the first nights in the cold, on the pavements of Porta Vittoria.

'They pay, O yes. But not one of them is normal,' and she gave a bitter smile.

The fact that the doctor was soon to arrive cheered her up, she took a brush and tidied her hair: I could not say which of those two before me was more painful to contemplate.

'O I could tell you a thing or two!'

'Some other time: I'm going down to let the doctor in.'

On the way up in the lift I briefed him. It turned out that Mary and I had not been wrong. He sounded the man's chest, rolled up his sleeve. The patient managed a few words.

'Take me . . . away . . .'

From the bag emerged the syringe, the rubber strip was tied just above the elbow, the veins stood out, Mary turned her head away.

'I'll come back tomorrow morning,' said the doctor. 'What he needs now is rest.'

We left the flat together. On my table the lamp still shone down that I had forgotten to turn out. But I gave in and watched the end of the film on television: the actress bore a resemblance to Ric's secretary, perhaps at that moment they were together in the hotel in Madrid, Francesca was bringing Emilia back here in her car, Jo sobbed on her bed, but how can our bodies betray us and ruin our best intentions, when to satisfy them should be the one certainty in a life of doubt, and if it is true that death rids us of this load, then we should embrace Her with relief, must explain to Doctor Y that this book is a ramp, that there is not one word of truth in it: I was on the point of catching the beginning of a different sort of truth, and the transmission was abruptly at an end.

I rose and switched off the television, but the emptiness around me was absolute now, a train whistled in

the distance, Mary would be lying down at her bene-
factor's side, it did not surprise me that she had turned
on her set: an announcer's tirade seeped feebly through
the floor.

Miriam, I called; all that wrong for nothing.

Beyond the balcony a luminous snake. The windows
of an express train raced by not a yard from me, the
explosive rush that is immediately deadened, the sub-
urbs like the edge of a stage-set, the lamps ringed like
targets, it was I who forced my way into the houses,
shook those uncurtained interiors, ghostly light-bulbs
swung at the end of their wires, I wed myself to the
misery of those walls, the breath that steams up the
windows of cafes, where the overhead wires end, where
the goods yards stretch, and then the few sticks of
furniture, soup in the plates, the doors of black-
despairing lavatories, the stricken door-posts, the
ghettoes of derelict factories.

Miriam, I called.

The voice of the newscaster sewed up the gaping rents.

When the hem of your coat is suddenly caught in
automatic doors, drawing you close after, it is already
a warning, a rehearsal for that wrench which will come
unannounced. More and more frequently now, I was
finding that I could not fall asleep unless I lay with
hands crossed on my chest. Grow accustomed to Her,
be familiar, and you are already learning not to fear
Her: but alarming events occurred, in my dreams, to
call such confidence in question.

Sometimes I described them to Emilia, so she could
give the right interpretation; they were signs, accord-

ing to her, of a hidden guilt complex. But their origin is to be traced further back, the roots go right into childhood; for example, an abyss would yawn between the lift and the floor, a gap, in reality, that does not measure an inch, my foot would slide on the edge just as I was entering the cabin itself, that was packed tight with people, and my whole body would plunge into the chasm, in an endless journey, and all the time no one would raise a finger to save me nor did I expect them to, I accepted that condemnation, shuddering only in expectation of the final thud, but the journey in the void was so long, the cabin was moving now, coming down on top of me, it is right, I told myself, it is right for this to happen, and all I feared as I was sucked down into darkness was the unspeakable pain at the shattering.

But our cowardice always leaves it to things to decide for us.

'I must do something, Emilia.'

'What?'

'I don't know, I must try and find out.'

'What you should try and do is to write a good book.'

I went right up to the refrigerator to look for the answer, the little cubes of ice that melt in the barley tang of whisky, the fingers gripping the icy glass.

'Listen, I have been thinking that . . .'

Too easy, I told her, to reach a state of awareness like mine, and then pretend that nothing has happened, live like the rest of the world, like my mother, Doctor Y, the girl downstairs.

Emilia lifted the newspaper again, to scan the headlines. If I was not familiar with her silences, I could have taken this for indifference, instead I began to wonder whether she did not consider the question a purely academic one and any discussion about it, pointless. With everything that is going on in this country, she seemed to be saying, laws trampled underfoot, shady deals tolerated, all the dirty things, the old things, you insist on digressing about the end we shall come to.

In fact, she lifted her eyes from the paper to say: 'I'm going to have a hot bath. Coming?'

The water poured reassuringly, the concerto was going to keep us company through the wide-open bathroom door, undoubtedly the smell of the bath salts was the most inviting thing there could be, late on a Sunday afternoon, and now as we talk with our faces surrounded by the foam (and Emilia's foot near that is as familiar as her hand to me), it is like a dialogue between two screens turned face to face.

'How goes it?' she smiles from her end of the bath.

'I feel I'm sprouting wings, just here, at my back.'

'You see?'

We were alone apart from Wolfgang Amadeus, and that phrase of his, known to us both, once more soothed the void left by an unanswerable question.

A feverish urge to act while there was time drove me on. I was the only one who treasured that notion which, coming from her, returned to her – I speak of my mother. This kept me mindful even of some dates – her birthday, her saint's day – which, before, I could never remember.

'But isn't this your saint's day?' I said to her over the phone.

She was flustered as she answered, trying to hide the pleasure it gave her, in the end she asked me to lunch, what was more I was to come with Emilia, I had to point out that it would take her too far away from her office, perhaps it would not be convenient.

'But you be sure and come,' her toneless voice commanded.

There was the usual traffic at the centre of town, lines of cars tied up at every cross-roads, and I noticed that I suffered this with less impatience. In Via Lanza engaged couples descended the steps of the City Hall, they had come to crave consent, as it is called, and they held hands with a smile that looked final, not knowing that they were barely at the beginning.

Contrariwise her bewilderment stems from finding that, after a lifetime spent on little duties, on daily tasks, she is alone with her own self in a silence that crushes her.

She is the one to say: 'What's wrong, aren't you well?'

'Why?'

'I have never seen you like this before: the look you have.'

Maybe it is because I am rather tired, I told her, because I never go out, I spent the whole morning at the typewriter; and this brings the old look of reproach to her face, because I live from day to day, with no profession and no regular salary. She has laid the table in the kitchen. If we were to sit down to eat in the living room, it would make strangers of us. Her utensils are a little worn, but set out in good order, the Singer occupies a corner, a household monster that is harmless now, I know the long history of every object here, suffering turned to neatness which the furnishings reflect, she will steal away on tiptoe, relieved to have left the sink clean, everything in its place, glad to have left no mark.

'Your brother went to Rome, he called at the Ministry, they told him that the pension will come through by May, can you believe that?'

As I ate, I tried to set her fears at rest, pointing that if they said so, it must be true, why doubt them, and I thought here I have come along empty-handed, I should have brought her flowers, a gesture to secure me peace of mind later on, when she was no longer there.

'It was to have been last year, first of all, then this November, and now they say May . . .'

She excused herself for not having wine, but it had been too cold for her to go out this morning, and her lodger is leaving inside a month, because he is to be transferred to another city, so she will have to find another one, and all because . . .

'Because your father packed and went!'

Something was burning on the stove: the hissing made her rise, now she grabs hold of the oven-cloth, her lips are drawn down, she looks like a geisha with her lambswool-edged slippers, the padded step, her hand trembles as she reaches for a fork, admit it now, I force myself to say, you had forgotten that today is your saint's day?

She smiles contritely: 'See this.'

She hands me the greetings card that her grandchildren have sent her, this year too, it is in the handwriting of the eldest, she puts it back in its place, pretending unconcern, her silence urges a model life on me, then at the dessert she bursts out with:

'You think I don't know? You've been seeing your father, haven't you?'

'Why, did somebody see me?'

'It doesn't take some one to see you: I know.'

I should assure her that I have too much to think about, at the moment, and anyway I do not even know where he lives, in what city, what street, instead I instinctively replied: 'Supposing I have?'

Her eyes flashed a moment, in the old way, then her head fell to one side, with the weight of the blow.

'You'll grow old, you others,' she said with a sigh, 'you'll know what it means.'

I wanted to shake her, take her by the shoulders and shout aloud that she must give up feeling so sorry for herself, open her eyes, learn what awaits us. Tell her that for months now I had been preparing myself for that sad occasion; that I had, all this while, been reading in her features hints of how we become plant or worm, seed or ant.

'I raised you all up: this is my reward.'

From my packet that is lying by my plate she slips out a cigarette, goes over to the stove to strike a match. I saw her face paling until it was transparent, her everlasting reproaches fading as composure returned. The dream of visiting her one day in the park of a villa set on the lake, her surrounded by her grandchildren, serene at last, was much more alien to me than that of her little hands gone rigid, the bloodless skin rubbed with spirits.

No sooner was I out of the house when that aggressive start of hers showed in the light of a good omen, the sign of a sure relapse. But I could be mistaken. Entering a telephone kiosk, I rang my brother at his office.

'But I don't understand,' he answered, 'I saw her myself, why, no time ago, she seemed buoyed up, to me.'

'You know how she is: she keeps worrying; she has that eternal fear of being left without any money. You've always given her your part, haven't you?'

A silence ensued and then came the brusque reaction: if anything it was I who had skipped the odd month, at least Mother had complained of this, I who had no children to raise, in any case it was ridiculous to worry about a matter like that, when she put it all away in the bank . . .

'What do you mean?'

He explained that last time he had been at her flat, just before travelling to Rome, he had found in a drawer of the sideboard which he was searching through for papers about the pension dispute, square in the middle of a heap of picture postcards—she was taking an after-lunch nap on the sofa—a savings bank account-book.

'But that just isn't possible. She never has a lira . . .'

'I saw it with my own eyes: there's almost a million marked up.'

I was ashamed to be engaged in that conversation, it was if a doctor was telling me in confidence that she was afflicted by a quite different illness, unbeknown to her. It humiliated me to learn just what she had brought herself to, to not trusting a living soul, but my dull resentment once more turned into comfort, I exonerated myself with regard to her. Waiting for the lights to change at Porta Vittoria, I had already left that thought well behind me.

'We should have her along,' said Emilia. 'Next Sunday you go and fetch her, and I'll put on a little lunch.'

'Perfect,' I said, 'you'll see how happy that makes her.'

We were in the by-pass that skirts the Shambles, headed for home, and I slowed down as we came to the cinema, opposite the illuminated posters. Emilia glanced out of the window.

'Look, was that not one you wanted to see?'

She got out to check the times of showing, I waited at the wheel, glad of an excuse for not working, I parked the car as soon as Emilia signed for me to join her, the film had just begun, and the moment I took my seat in the dark of that smoky interior, coats on our knees, I let myself be carried away, as I used to be, by the shapes projected before our eyes, a wonderful, unbelievable tale simply asked us to give up all our reservations, so that, for an hour, neither of us said a word.

Probably it was the light thrown off by the enormous screen or, more likely, its fading as a darker background came in: the silence of the stalls could not have been more complete, it was almost ecstatic, and that unquestioning readiness, quite unnatural in the first place, failed me.

At my side I sensed rather than saw Emilia's profile, my field of vision encompassed the dark shapes of all the heads and only now could I observe how motionless they were: not a muscle twitched in those faces, suddenly I caught a little gurgle from low down in my left side, some blockage that had cleared itself at once, and as the rest of my body held steady, that little physiological happening bulked all the larger in importance, an underground explosion heard outside the tunnel, my elbow rested on the arm of my seat, my forearm lay in Emilia's lap, my hand touching

hers, and what I was watching now struck me as all
but senseless, the mouths of the actors moved without
making any sound, even our own breathing was
inaudible, a pink glow was shed on an amphitheatre of
puppets and with a catch of fear I saw that not only
I but all of us were mummified there, Emilia's fingers
were cold clay, I did not dare lower my eyes to confirm this nor turn them any other way: it is this, then,
a show going on outside of us, I closed my eyes an
instant and once again that little burst came, a bubble
collapsing in an artery, I saw it plain before my eyes
while the objects and people upon the screen grew
blurred, I must shout out, I thought, warn them while
there is time, but I was incapable of making any
gesture, chained to that seat like the others, black
sacks stuffed with paper, fossilized husks in a great
silence, it is the dawn, I thought, a cloud of bluish
smoke hovered over the heads, moreover it was easy
for me to distinguish whose they were: they belonged
to Miriam, my mother, there was Doctor Y, and then
Denyse, Jo, Emilia at my side, Edo's hand like a leaf,
its surface dotted over with kidney spots, its spiky
form, grown lean with time, the hand of someone
out of distant, prehistoric times, we travelled on together, swallowed by the light, the eye-sockets emptied
now, our clothes hanging over decomposed limbs, I
was not in the least concerned by what was happening
on the screen, there was no longer any need to understand it, an undreamt-of joy flowed out from the
narrow slot where my body had sunk down, they have
gone away, it murmured, they have all gone away,
and the cardboard figures looked on impassive, their
necks rigid in the gloom, do you see, it repeated, it is
nothing, before us stretched an immense plain, white

and black lozenge-tiles of a floor once seen, I am safe, you thought, I went forward boldly, I trampled a horizon of cobblestones, between converging walls towards something which slowly rose in the distance, go on, they ordered, go on, the smell of wax at the foot of the turbine, the black enamel on the different pieces of machinery, it was strange that the direction-finders no longer brought anguish, the sucking of the pumps, the tubes vanished into whirling, aseptic chambers, an obscure force seemed to be loosed by the underground ducts as they overflowed from a fault in the mechanism, a sob braked the spinning of the flywheels, the needles fell back in the baroscopes, we are only at the beginning, come forward, a sudden upsurge of pulleys, levers, gauges, rigid handles. And still weightless I proceeded towards the last hallways of nothingness, my gaze now piercing clean through the skulls lined along the seats, and there was the shock, suddenly, of a prayer granted: I caught sounds outside our range, I made out the invisible, drawn as an insect is drawn to a bright light, but still fighting against the possible revelation I was not prepared for.

I was startled by Emilia's voice.

'Hey—you don't want to see the whole thing through again from the beginning, do you?'

Strong winds, they have announced, along the whole arc of the Alps. Even the blind-slats were shivering this morning, and the porter's voice over the internal phone answered Emilia to tell her there has been a breakdown in the heating system. So much the worse, I said to her, for Doctor Y. Once she had gone out,

I dressed hurriedly. To be free to wander about is one of the few privileges of my state, but I set myself an objective every time: today I was going to purchase a barometer.

Our unrest, by itself, prepares the traps we at once try to escape from: a deadline, a promise, a journey. It is when this happens that we go back to worshipping idleness as the only hope, the simple flowing-by of days. But a natural law drives us again, and again, to this senseless game, between sun and shade, where we are pursuing what we have just shaken off.

Perhaps, I was surprised to find myself thinking, it was like that with Miriam: desire alternating with shame. Could it be the same with Emilia tomorrow? Then it is one force which determines this interplay of contradictions? I crossed the street. The air bore creakings and thuds. The railway arch. Pizzeria, cooked meats. And then Her again, as inescapable punishment, an obsession I had to free myself from. Not quite the pain that strangles you, but rot in the teeth that every passing day accentuates, the dull throbbing in the gums which tells decay, plague at the root: She is not easy to live with, I could conclude, hoping all the while to be rid of Her. The realization that She is for ever present had stimulated me at first; now it threatened to paralyse me.

'I never dreamt,' I told the shopkeeper, 'they would be so dear.'

He explains that these are the best, English barometers, and that they do not stock the cheap sort, I'll think about it, I answered: the bus was already drawing up at the stop, I got on just in time, the hem of my coat was trapped in the automatic doors, and yet being in this position did not feel at all like a warning, I was so exultant at having escaped, because you want a great deal of luck to get away from Her like this, at the last moment, slip through Her fingers, the ticket-collector watched me apprehensively, I don't give a damn, I wanted to tell him, try again, I felt I was the stronger, try and get my shoulders in, this time, but at the next stop more passengers came on to push me further along the bus.

I got down in Largo Augusta. I did not know I was to have a lucky morning. At the newstand where I halted a man stood gazing, abstractedly, at a cover hung out on the garish side: a photo-image of a woman in a *négligé*, pointing a gun, and his face expressed nothing, it bore only the sullen look of someone planning a crime, he made as if to walk on but gave up, hypnotized by that pose. I looked in my turn, when he had finally torn himself away, I studied the woman's gaze and then I turned back to the man who was getting down off the pavement but I could not guess what had passed between the two. Only when I was about to move on, with my eyes still on that cover, did I see that it was Mary.

It was her, photographed in colour, the garment open at the breasts, she was not easily recognizable because of a red wig which cascaded to her shoulders.

'Let me have that book,' I said, holding out the money already counted.

It was a trophy for Emilia, which, meantime, I stuck into my pocket; back in the flat we would look it through together, this yarn in the erotico-detective style, you should introduce her to Doctor Y, Emilia would laugh, she could pose for your story, in fact, why don't you photograph her yourself?

I do not like it when Emilia jokes like this, even if

it is from an instinct of self-defence. I stopped in my tracks, a horn-blast made me jump. If I could once superimpose Mary's image on Miriam's, I would have freed myself. Perhaps. I did not dare put my hopes on it, but it might be a way. In Corso Europa I caught myself looking for Doctor Y's window in the glass fronts of the high buildings. Fine, the first part: he repeated. It was eleven o'clock, I walked with the truculence of a deserter. But if I had come to this, to bowing to a vile contract, it means there are other, quite different possibilities of self-abasement, at this point I wondered just how far you could go in performing acts you did not believe yourself capable of, moreover I had forgotten that, in the end, my masterpiece would be made to look ridiculous by the illustrations, by nudity snapped in dim-witted poses between four walls somewhere.

My hand, thrust into my overcoat pocket, squeezed the book, it fraternized with Mary, sent comforting messages to consciousness. From the church of San Calimero a funeral procession was wending that forced the traffic to a crawl. Your prayers, said the bannerol, for this good soul, and it would be refreshing to read the words, just once, your prayers for this bastard, but death redeems a man in the eyes of the living, and I observed those who had been close to him holding the cords put there, as punishment, at the four corners of the bier, their names printed in gold on violet ribbons, all the paraphernalia that the end of a man comes to. I turned into Via Lamarmora. On the wall someone has written: disarm the police.

Emilia had not come back yet. I laid the table and sat down to wait for her. It was strange that she had forgotten to warn me. There: the telephone rang.

'It's me— who's speaking?'

First Aid, said the voice, your wife's here, don't panic, an accident with her car, an abyss of dread opened before me, I noted how it all seemed so natural, an arm, the voice explained, nothing serious.

'Just wait, I'm on my way.'

I rang for a taxi, struggled into my coat as I ran down the stairs. The trip to the hospital went on for ever. So She could introduce Herself like this, too, strike with no explanations given, in fact this is probably the way it will happen, She is so sure we shall acquiesce, and immediately. Before the entrance they were drawing out a stretcher from an ambulance, I raced over: it was a youth, his face all swollen. Emilia was in the waiting room, seated on a wheel-chair, her face lit up as soon as she caught sight of me.

'See what I've managed to do?'

She was still wearing her coat, she supported her left elbow with her hand, a shiver went right through her from time to time.

'I think it's broken. They are going to take an X-ray. It's nothing, you'll see.'

She was making an effort to reassure me but escaped she had: a car had cut in from the left, on the big square just before home, its bonnet had rammed right into her door, she thought she was going to faint with the pain while they were pulling her out on the other side, keep calm, I said, don't get excited, her teeth were chattering with the shock, at last a male nurse arrived and pushed Emilia along to the X-ray room, I went with her, the process of taking off her things made her cry out two or three times, once bared, her arm was a fearful sight, the bone out of joint, the limb no longer seemed to belong to her as they laid it out on one corner of the X-ray table, she turned her gaze on me as cries and sobbing were heard coming from the room opposite, muffled by the doors and, so, much more doleful, will it hurt me? in ten minutes it will be all over, the male nurse put in, lucky that the break is a fresh one, see? I forced myself to cheer her up, the man who crashed into you knew you play tennis, he picked your left arm, but I was trying to make it bearable for myself, in fact.

Emilia was laid out on a hospital cot, she was ashen, the surgeon examined the slide, my hand, thrust into my overcoat pocket, came into contact with half-naked Mary again, another doctor was bent over the wash-basin. They patted her arm here and there and the arm jerked as if it had been touched by a powerful electric current, there was an acute howl from Emilia, her body arched up on the cot, there, that's it done, said the surgeon, the plaster-impregnated bandages emerged steaming from the container, were already being wound on, from her wrist to her shoulder, I was struck by the readiness with which accidents are accepted, as if everything that had gone before had no other purpose than to lead up to this mishap, and yet that itself is no more than a simple warning.

'You will have to stay perfectly still for the first few days,' the surgeon advised.

The man who had crashed into Emilia was leaving the dressing station himself, his forehead all plaster where the shattered windscreen had cut it. On the way home in the taxi, it struck me as unnatural that the people and the streets registered no change. This must be how the dead look at us; deeply hurt by the show of healthiness, and Emilia seemed to feel just that, as she stared out morosely at the avenue we were passing along. I could imagine what depressed her: knowing she would be handicapped for forty days, would have to rely on my manual lack-of-skill, condemned to inactivity.

She shivered with the cold, her overcoat only half on: but you've had nothing to eat, she remembered, and I've left the keys stuck there in the dashboard, you'll see how the car is, it's all crumpled up, don't talk, you'll only tire yourself, you've to go to bed now, I ordered, I shall make you a lovely hot cup of tea, I tried to play the incident down and, at the same time, find a meaning for it: I asked myself whether nothing happens by chance and, if so, what was the significance of this accident, how did it stand to what was awaiting us, or does mere chance govern these fruitless experiences which the least bit of luck would spare us. I would now go to the chemist's, then see that a breakdown van removed our car, and then write out a report for the insurance people. I was organizing a retreat, I calculated the strength of my remaining forces, I regrouped them.

When the cabin of the lift jerked to a halt at the ground floor, it was Mary who came out of it: her arms were laden with furs.

'My father's coming tonight,' she smiled. 'He'd better not see these.'

She struggled out through the lift door, she saw the plaster on Emilia's arm as it protruded from the unbuttoned coat, she asked about it, her regret and sympathy could have been sincere.

'If you need help, don't hesitate,' and she vanished

with her soft load down the steps to the basement.

Her flesh shone as if it were lit from inside, and I did not dare even to touch her: her skin, her eyes, her hair, her eyebrows, I felt some mysterious force flowing out from her, this must be how the Virgin appears in visions, and Miriam kept her beautiful, spoilt mouth half-open, in her innocence, what brings you back? said my gaze, but it was sweet to drown in those murky pupils, the taste of her saliva, now that her whole figure was revealed to me, she rose up slowly before me, seemed to hover in air, and came towards me, her body magnified enormously, I have my case with me, she spoke now: I've left my people, you can see that I've done it.

My hand worked her knee round unceasingly, vulgarity and sweetness met in her to make the irresistible, what I could never give up: . . . die, repeated Miriam, my finger-tips attacked where her stockings ended, I found my fetishes still intact, unspoilt by time: the suspender-belt, the buckle, the lace gathered up on the navel, a vision that never stops exciting you for the way the fabric bulges, of the briefs, the whiteness of the skin, hair and saliva, the hand-grips, for the coffin, yes, dear, like that: what have you to say now? the odour that is exhaled, triumphant, and still I pronounced that name with the voluptuousness of a fruit, I breathed in her palate, her case with her few things was still in the hall, don't say that, don't say that, she implored, throwing back her head, her case reflected in the mirror, you must not be afraid, and she breathed out all the pleasure that filled her breast, the roots of her hair beaded with sweat, your tongue, she begged, her eyes shining in a face gone leaden pale, the fight we entered was with ourselves, powerless before the body's inadequacy, while a violent wave shook us, making the slightness of the organs unbearable, the parts she wanted bared, flesh tissue stretched by that furious urging, look, she intimated, through clenched teeth, look, I don't know what I'm doing, what I'm saying, her arrogance bowed down, demanded punishment, more, she commanded, more, and I rolled with her, frightened by this delirium we would soon hold no longer, I broke off to fill my eyes with her hips, her legs, the opening in the groin, be quiet, she implored, be quiet, a love-machine ready for everything base, mine for the first time, a surge of life that was about to explode, and a new outrage inflamed her impatience, mine, like that, she exclaimed, go right home; a brief beating of wings and we fell over, grappling, into no man's land.

Look Her straight in the eye, I told myself: it is there that you will find what you have to learn, how to be familiar with Her, how to change the idea you have had of Her completely. You should be able to contemplate Her with the same detachment you have as you watch, from twenty-five thousand feet up, the clouds breaking into idle shrapnel over the ocean. And if I came to love Her really, this timeless anguish, then I would hold the most powerful of talismans in my hands.

In reality what I feared, more keenly with each day's passing, was that She might arrive before I was ready to give myself up, before I had found the courage to tell Emilia how my story with Miriam had ended.

'Have you been awake long?' she asked on opening her eyes.

She complains that when, in a few days time, she has to take up her work at the Centre again, she will have lost the faculty of responding to the alarm.

We have had to change places in bed, so that the plaster will not come between us, and she says with a smile that it is the hollow I have made in the mattress that induces all this sleepiness.

I raised the blind: February's sun was winning through the mist. By the sink I found a pile of dirty plates and glasses.

'How do you feel?'

Her shoulder looks minute where it emerges from that white armour. I brought her milk and biscuits: I had just begun to dress when the door-bell rang.

'Can I be of any help?'

I was wondering how Emilia would take this offer, when, recognizing Mary's voice, she called to her to come in, greeted her warmly, invited her to sit down on the bed.

'You see, I have to go out and do some shopping . . .'

She explained that she was having to cook for her father, as he refused to eat in restaurants, and so, if we needed anything, we only had to say what and she would buy it, even cook it, for us.

'It would be too bad if we had to ask that of you,' Emilia smiled in amusement.

Mary sat wide-legged, careless rather than proud of what she showed, and apart from this there was nothing in her that betrayed the way she made her living, except for her look which was the selfsame one that the girl on the cover had.

'And your arm doesn't hurt?'

She looked at Emilia admiringly, she says that she would die at the mere thought of a fracture, and Emilia studies her in turn, aware that this present familiarity is rarely allowed the married woman, her gaze telling both simple curiosity and the sociologist's interest.

'What about your friend,' I said, 'that man?'

'He's gone,' she answered gaily. 'It was only a passing crisis.'

She went on to tell us how she had been to have the cards read, she goes twice a week, and Madame Ester had warned her that it would be better if she did not see that man again.

'Do you know Madame Ester? I'll give you the address: she's pure magic.'

The internal phone summoned me: Luigino announced that a registered letter had arrived. I finished dressing and went down to the hall. When I came back up, I found Mary was busying herself in the little kitchen. She had tied on an apron and was in the middle of washing up, talking loud and merry to Emilia all the while: you would have thought this was her prime diversion.

'What's going on?' I murmured.

Emilia shrugged: she had tried to stop her but without success. Now we would have to put up with Mary's zeal, also because it was, all in all, an excellent idea. But probably my good humour came from my having just received a cheque in payment for that last story of mine.

'I was explaining to your wife that my father imagines I'm at the shop . . .'

Everything was plain: the beauty parlour in town, where she used to go and earn her wages, thank heaven she is putting him on a train that afternoon, because these two days with her father have cost her a packet, not to mention the nightmare possibility that he may take one of her calls.

'And yesterday he comes out with: now what on earth are you doing, girl, with three dressing-gowns!'

As if the story concerned some other person, we all three laughed aloud. I felt I had wronged her in procuring that book the day before, although Mary in the role of drudge was quite unconvincing. I decided not to show it even to Emilia. This gave me a feeling of magnanimity, of satisfaction, even although I saw full well that I would do no work that morning.

'Are you going out?'

'I'm going to the hospital to pick up your X-ray.' I leant over Emilia's pillow and whispered the advice. 'Don't believe everything she tells you.'

My decision seemed to put Mary out: her salutation was tinged with disappointment. What on earth could she be thinking? I had taken it all along that she cultivated us to have a respectable cover that hardly anyone else would have been ready to provide. So it should nor worry me much if my leaving her alone with Emilia made her feel humbled, reduced to being a kind of maidservant.

A dazzling light played on the road: I had already observed that awareness of Her hits me more readily on days like this, when the sun blazes, when the light glorifies the most ordinary things, when the eye focuses, sharply, the outline of rubbish.

A lemonade bottle, for example, on a second floor windowsill at the Surgeons' Institute. Wide entrances, gloomy corners, courtyards with all their dinginess exposed. An empty bottle, the emaciation of the ironwork, crumbling of brick. Nurses chased by, in groups. Doctors stood on the corner where the tobacconist's is, with hats and gloves, white shirt peeping from overcoat, discussing promotion like officers of a garrison. In the basement marked 'X-ray Section', as I waited at the desk for the sister to come back with the slide, I was struck by the gaze of the people sitting on the out-patients' bench, a gaze that asks for pity, convinced of the end but not wanting to linger and suffer too long.

'One hundred and forty-one,' called out the sister.

I held out the ticket and took the slide. It was a while since I had taken Emilia flowers. I would have to remember on the way home. For once our day was reversed: she in bed and I running errands. You know, darling: a fracture with attendant detachment of the condyle of the humerus, tearing of ligaments, blotches, greyish or white, one part, a hazy black, dense with secrets, no one cares to acknowledge themselves in this negative held up to the light. I even doubted that those bones, newly set, too fragile to last, were Emilia's.

There is that grassy slope running at the foot of the Spanish bastions in Via Filippetti, where the open sky invites to meditation. If it is a lucky day, I will get some creative start there, isolate the nucleus of a novel, accelerate the particles making up my stories, and they are the moments, these, when I let Her sit beside me, without fear.

No I could once more offer Her a place on the bench, for I felt life beating so strong in me that, far from being afraid of Her, I provoked Her, challenged Her to a barbaric trial by fire. Come, I said to Her, come now if you have the courage to. Even the Spanish walls make fascinating reading: I looked for a sign in the brickwork, a spiral from nature, some miscroscopic remains within the complex of buildings in new stone, and the sight of history peeping out between the hedge and the municipality's litter basket (the last warning), gratified me.

I stared at the ice-crust around the fountain. Even the stones on the hard ground shone like coins. A few feet away an old man rummaged under a bench in search of cigarette-butts. Show yourself, I said to Her, take me now, be brave.

I knew, though: She never comes when She is called. She knows this is the only way we have of showing our contempt. The old man drew nearer. I felt the sacrilegious urge to hammer a stained-glass window to pieces, or the crust frozen over the water, or the tough stone of heaven, the perfect blue which offends the dead.

I'm ready, I repeated, what are you waiting for?

With his stick he scraped under the bush, he wore torn half-gloves of wool, there was a package there, I saw him straightening with a grimace that told disgust, his face was ridged by two shaggy eyebrows, I felt as if they had grazed me, that straggly beard repelled me, the long metal-stiff hair, I knew there were still many things I had to do, but what happened sent a shiver through me, because the old man had kept worrying the paper wrapping with the point of his stick, the string binding the package had gone slack, something appeared, a small, formless animal thing, a slimy, pink huddle like a jelly-fish, yes, but with something of the bat about it, the old man shook his head, don't look, I told Emilia, there are still some old houses at the corner of the avenue, crushed by new buildings, and I was sure this unclean thing had come from there, I felt I should inform the police, but the old man had moved off with his bundle, revolted by that uncanny discovery, there was nothing for it but to follow him, find out who he was. I rose up from the bench and, keeping down my nausea, looked again: how do you account for it, I asked myself, in the heart of a metropolis, and I became aware that moment that I had never considered what end awaited the dozens of beings that a city rejects each day, bloody heaps washed down the sewers, I could not tear myself from that horrible sight which the old man's stick had happened to turn up, as if more of life lay in death, as if Miriam had come back to repeat in a voice that did not want to be heard: I'm afraid that I'm pregnant . . .

I had to know; the old man was moving away, bent double, my cheeks tingled with the cold, as I walked, I felt a slight pain above my left knee, and everything I had experienced to then lost all significance before what awaited me. I was saying goodbye to the things I had loved, with easy step I followed that old man as he hobbled up Via Ripamonte, passed through an entry, a wide courtyard, a heap of coal, an Alsatian tugged at its chain, I pushed open a glass-paned door with a hanging over it, as I followed him, I caught the scent of sweet orange peel gently stewing on the stove, the old man had opened up the grate, his head was lost to sight in the burning glow of the embers, listen, I said to him, I must know, I'm doing everything to know, he took a shovel-full of coal and tossed it into the grate, he held out his hands, sheathed in the half-gloves, to the heat that radiated, this is the season when more are dying, he finally spoke, when cold or the wind cuts them off, because as many as eighty a day are brought in by the vans, you don't know, you can't even imagine, what it's like to be municipal grave-digger for twelve years, but that's just it, I almost shouted, that's why I've come, you must tell me everything.

Oh? says the old man, what is it you want to know? He has brought out a pipe and fills it now, quite unaware of the miraculous chance that has set him in my way, by now it's turned into a job like any other, he explains, with rubber gauntlets on that reach to your elbows, almost a clean trade, with mechanical aids and plastic sacks, but in the old days you had corpses that rotted the first few days and smelt to high heaven, can I have a match? he drew in on his pipe, what is it you want to know? everything: I insisted, there was a camp-bed by the stove, he pointed out a bench where I could sit, well then, the coffin lasts a year, a year and a half, if the wood is good and sound, then it caves in, he ran his fingers through his filthy hair as he tried to remember, at the time of an epidemic, when the mercury sinks in the barometer or with the first chills of autumn, it was like digging trenches, and the best soil for it is one with sand and gravel, otherwise if it is clayey, it doesn't rot them, but the worms? I broke in.

His smile turned to coughing, he cleared his throat: what worms? people just imagine the worms, I sent him a look of gratitude, I could scarcely believe that neither annelida nor platyhelminthes would feed on me, because they can't get down more than a foot or so, and seeing the graves are at least five feet deep, but what is it that you're so keen to know?

Go on, I ordered: only the repugnance I felt at his look stopped me from hugging him, I was grateful to him in my mother's name, in Emilia's, Edo's, for all those I could not bear to think of as being assaulted in their sleep and befouled, I knew now that we should have no fear because down below there is peace, only water trickling in the earth's veins, especially if the plots have been turned over not long before, fresh earth and gravel to let the rain filter right down to the depths, he rose up and put a little pot on the stove, of course, he answered, there are the exhumations: still, I've always refused the mask, you breathe badly enough in those tight digging spaces, but the bones, you should see them, picked clean and washed, they ring out like bells, they're a sight.

The walls of the hut were bare, except for a saint's image stuck up with a drawing pin: and when there is a re-burial, he said, you see them there as we left them no time ago, hands crossed on their chests, only the eye has dissolved, it's always the eye that goes first, but all clean and simple, oh I've seen a few in twelve years I can tell you, and turning his bristling eyebrows towards the stove, he lapsed into an obstinate silence, as if he regretted speaking. It was only then that I noticed Her sitting beside him, Her unmistakable stench, but after, I wanted to ask him, what happens after?

After what? She said.

A painting—that is Emilia in profile as she sleeps, with the rug framing her chin; so vulnerable in her certainties, so open to any blow – I stay there watching her.

But my gaze makes her shift position and, finally, open her eyes.

'How do you feel?'

'But where have you been?'

A foggy Sunday, the afternoon strangely white, and boundless. Her skin, the smell of wool, the big sweater covering Emilia to her hips.

'Here: I haven't budged.'

Only in idleness do we belong to ourselves. A record with bell ringing, that is at once swallowed up in the silence. On holidays this could be a hospital district: not one sound from the courtyards, the desire of evasion in everyone, and today there are not even the shouts of the boys from the football pitch.

'This arm of mine,' she bursts out with, and changes position.

Her irony has been tempered since she was forced to keep still, or rather it has switched targets: from others to herself. It is in constant play now, to keep her from falling into the pathetic.

'Do you know that Mary is called Cettina?'

You see, she explained, her real name is Maria Concetta: yesterday morning what with one question and another she has come to know a great deal. First and foremost, that the girl had come to Milan, after getting into trouble in her own village, and not even knowing who the man was that had put her in the family way, one morning she took the train and goodbye.

'Do you find the subject so interesting?' I broke in.

'Oh no, much too elementary.'

Then a girl friend who was already leading that life at Milan had taken her to a doctor, lent her the money necessary, and then, to pay off the debt, or so she says, she had joined the ranks; at the beauty parlour in the underground she had stayed no more than a week, Mary says she could not breathe, she was not used to working underground, but in fact she was trying to find some justification for selling herself on the pavement in the first place, a bare six months have passed since she began operating from home by telephone, and she sends money to her people every month, a few more years of this and she will retire, she will go back to her own town and open a shop, because she knows no one here and she does not relish the idea of having a pimp who rows you if you stop to have a coffee, the most amazing thing, Emilia said, is her coldness, her readiness to yield to everything we call immoral: she took a cigarette and lit it from mine, there's probably some character-type trauma at the root of it.

I could no longer follow her account of it. The moment drew near for me to confess the last detail to her. I had to involve her in my obsession if I was to get free of it. I had not moved beyond the face of this father whom neither of us had seen and who, perhaps, had never even arrived, considering how easily and naturally Mary could tell any lie, a Southerner's face which I grafted on to that of Miriam's father, the features set in the cast of his own poverty-stricken village, no longer the sea of olives, the red clods, the turning vane over the artesian well, the lime and mortar dwelling, nor the spice tang from the pines, the lentisk, the berries, nor the sirocco attacking the uplands, I was entering, along with the few others returning, the country town Mary had run away from, and before her, Miriam's father, all the reasons for his sudden flight, still there, unchanged: the hand-cart with the bellows torn to ribbons, the chairs out in the lane, a place slumped down on itself, at this time of day more battered than baroquely picturesque, the bare-brick walls of new habitations, the low buildings, the embroidery on the balconies, streams of dirty water running over imperial stones, and down below, the plain of the Tavoliere stretching vast, without end, to be seen from a terrace which no one looks over now, petrified as they are, across from their cathedral, rooted to the seats of the Men's Club, awaiting the end, and in the same way that images spurt and teem, with fierce masturbation, I saw connections, took in whole chains of related effects, thunderstruck myself to find how infinite the ramifications were: Mary and the package that the old man had disturbed, its gruesome contents, my father will kill me if he comes to know, Miriam said with real fear while Emilia goes on narrating, and the thick mist swirls at the panes, Mary tried to make a place for herself between us, call me Cettina, said her doll-like body, but there was that stick, the point of it fumbling in the package, and Miriam advancing to overwhelm everything else.

'I want a cat,' Emilia concluded, 'a cat just for myself.'

I was aware of something incestuous in the tenderness which I put into it, and in the wariness with which she received me, her stiff arm lying across two pillows.

One chapter was still to write, and I had only a few days left before the final deadline set by Doctor Y. With Emilia at home, I had not progressed by a single line: it was as if the subject of the book demanded complete and private abandon from me, something that her mere presence was enough to inhibit.

Emilia decided to start work again this very day. I took her up to her Centre by car. In the afternoon I have my final notes to work up, and, as I do this, I taste such satisfaction at finding myself alone and undisturbed once more that I am almost ashamed of it: this pleasure of giving myself up to fantasy in time to a well-tempered piano, and all as if nothing had happened meanwhile.

Going over the last few chapters, I have had to add a touch or two, minute but precious details. Of its kind, this strikes me as an excellent bit of work: it exploits, for example, my discovery of the erotic charge that is latent in womanly confidences, at the point where the married woman reveals to a young, unmarried one just what obscene acts she was driven to for love—this word that Doctor Y dislikes—with the growing excitement seen in the woman listening, a conversation of inviting questions and ambiguous answers, the spectacle, finally, of corruption working quietly and, therefore, so much more voluptuously, indelible memories of Miriam, the pretty ways of her inexpert hands, and where I strove hardest to imitate the real and outrage the most fundamental sense of shame, the boldness of the attempt compensated me for the perversity in it, I congratulated myself for the way in which, through two womanly mouths, I was mocking the law and my own good name.

And as I was writing I did not dream that this was to be the last time I deceived myself. At a quarter to five only a few pages stood between me and the end. Now all that I had to do was pile it on thick as the last act rose to crescendo, I felt certain that Emilia would not read the typescript again and that released my libido, it played over the page in new variations, in the vulgarity of the words, in an exciting urgency that spilled from the sheet and poured all round, over the room and over my past until the consciousness of my own vileness turned into a sense of fulfilment.

The concerto was at an end, only the tapping from my portable broke the silence. I drew out the last quarto sheet bearing the words 'the end'. I did not ask myself what that experience had taught me (not counting some vague pointers to the pornographic art), nor did I propose to. The tension of it had engrossed me and, thanks to that, I could put away the question which, some months earlier, had occurred, suddenly, like a virus in healthy tissue.

Tomorrow, I thought, I will go to Doctor Y's and hand him the text. Mary must have gone out: her phone went on ringing. I too had sold myself.

'Yes', answered Emilia, 'who's speaking?'

I was helping her to undress, peeling her sleeve from the plaster-cast, and I glanced at the clock, alarmed at the lateness of the hour.

'No, he's not here. But what's happened?'

She mouthed the name 'Josephine' to me.

'But how did that come about?'

We had heard nothing more of her or Ambro for over a month and this call, to judge from Emilia's frown, boded no good.

'No, I don't think so. Hold on, and I'll get him to talk to you.'

Emilia put the receiver into my hand.

Jo's voice was wild with panic: they had quarrelled that afternoon, and Ambro, after a stormy exit, had not come back home yet, she had thought he might have been at our place, she was phoning all their friends, she apologized but she was worried in case he did something foolish, perhaps she had even woken us up.

'No,' I said, 'we've just got in from the theatre, we were getting ready for bed.'

I asked if he had packed a bag, she replied that he had not even taken his pipe, her ingenuity was touching, he had walked out straight, raging like a madman, nothing so violent had ever taken place between them.

'I've phoned the ambulance service to enquire, I don't know what else to do.'

'Don't be afraid,' I said, 'you'll see. Everything will turn out alright tomorrow.'

I spoke the usual words of comfort, and, really, what Jo needed was some one by her. It was Emilia who suggested I go: as a friendly act which I owed to Ambro too.

'Perhaps you'd better go by yourself.'

Her shoulder joint ached, and anyway she would not have known what to say to her. I rang Jo back, to tell her I was coming. I was not looking forward to it myself, but the idea that I might be useful helped me over my embarrassment.

A maid was waiting at the outside door, we mounted the steps to the first floor together, Madam was telephoning, I was shown into the library. A pendulum clock struck half past one. When Jo appeared, I had the unpleasant impression that she had just changed for my benefit, as if I had been lured to an equivocal sort of meeting. Her hand, too, held mine longer than necessary.

'Sit down. It's kind of you to come like this.'

I glanced around the room as if looking for some mark of a quarrel, but the traces, if any, were probably to be found in the bedroom, it had happened at three in the afternoon, you know, the usual things, Jo said, relating the incident, he said to me: don't imagine I can put up with living like this much longer, because the truth is Ambro no longer leads the life of a husband, he is simply a shadow who comes and goes at will, then suddenly the explosion, he grabbed the phone and hurled it at her, luckily the boys were out with the governess, will you have something to drink? Josephine broke off to ask, she passed me a glass before I could answer, her own breath already smelt of whisky, I've taken you away from Emilia, she joked, but I'm desperate, I don't know who to turn to, you did the right thing, I smiled, and my eyes went to the library itself, the books lined on the shelves in the half-light from shaded lamps, books from which Ambro distilled his wisdom, and what's more she was saying, you are a writer, you can understand these things, what are you writing at the moment? nothing, I said, short stories for the papers, and your novel? she let her legs slide wide, not caring what I could see, I'm sure he has another woman in his life, she rose up, took a few steps, hugging her own shoulders, a keen wave of perfume went out from her, she stopped in front of my chair: I can say this to you because I trust you, said Jo as if she were talking to herself: he hasn't touched me in months, how can we go on like this?

144

On the couch, in a half-opened parcel, I could make out the advance copies of Ambro's new book. Unquestionably, if I could have flicked through to the page or the pages concerning myself, I would have found them more interesting than this private narration of Jo's, but it was not the moment for that, however much at ease I felt for having come, my presence sealing, as it were, a pact of mutual support, in a time of crisis. What I could glimpse was a sober top cover, a stack of paper-back spines, some letters of the title, and Jo fell back again into the armchair opposite, how did this come about? she repeated in that adorable accent of hers.

I had lost the drift of the conversation, I swallowed down a mouthful of whisky, Jo's slender legs moved restlessly, in search of a comfortable lie, nothing brings greater disappointment, I remembered having read, than involving yourself in other people's affairs, in short, I was determined not to express an opinion, not to side with one or the other, a little drop more, she half-asked, filling up my glass again, because I believe a man, come on, let's hear what you have to say, a man, she went on, should always want to make love to me, and never come to an end, don't you think?

Two pale blue globes rolled no distance away from my face: I was certain, in myself, that I had never desired her, and never less than now, or perhaps, she continued, her eyes still fixed on mine, you imagine I'm no good in bed?

'I think you must be wonderful,' I answered gravely.

As she stubbed out her cigarette, her face came nearer mine. I was afraid that she expected some gesture on my part, admittedly it was not because she had invited me that I was there with her in her house at that so late hour, or perhaps she expected a remark that would console her in her wounded vanity, and although Jo did not attract me, her vulnerability linked up with my obsession, I felt her to be, in spite of herself, tainted by that selfsame thought of the end, and it was the whiteness of her skin, her eternal mood of panic, the freckles that her make-up hid, her defence-less look, perhaps she would have done it just to feel alive, there on that couch, with me or with anyone else, two strokes echoed from the hall, imperiously they brought the absent Ambro to mind, I wondered where he was and how long this waiting would go on for, perhaps he is with Mary, I thought, the idea amused me, and, after all, he had never been in our house, no fear of discovery could have deterred him from such a visit, or perhaps even with Emilia, I remembered the looks he had given her that day by the sea, but right now Emilia had a broken arm and eyes that were weighed down with sleep.

'Is that Ambro's book?' I asked, pointing to the copies.

Jo did not reply, her hands to her head, and long minutes passed in silence. We were watching over some one deceased, suddenly the field of vision opened out, Jo's pubic mound, blonde-haired, shaved by a safety razor, empty associations, reminders, a dark stain on the cushion-cover, still damp, perhaps gold dust clinging to the nipple's brown ring, a creaking from the book-shelves, I felt Miriam pressing from a long way off, coming forward in the half-light, and I began to fear this, I must go, I told myself, but could not be resolute, my place empty in the bed, Emilia, the unfailing tenderness that wakes in me as I lay

146

myself down by her slumbering body, until Jo's shoes fell soundlessly from the feet she had drawn up on her chair.

'Say something, please.'

I could not make out the walls of the room, the ceiling itself had gone higher, we stood opposite one another in the frozen amazement with which two escalators cross on their different ways, like dummies, ourselves, ecstatic, completely lived-out, my voice is saying: everything will come right, you'll see, and Jo bursts out sobbing.

'Go away,' she wept, 'go away.'

Her whole body shook, a sight I had already witnessed as unbearable; it was trying to involve me, it suggested pain of a kind which, once before, I had been powerless to soothe, come on now, don't do that, we call life pleasure, love, hope, when really it is grief, bewilderment, loneliness, how well you talk, she would have said, and we should learn to taste a joy with anxiety, too, knowing it is not to last, clench your fist, said the nurse: a rush of warmth and the blood gushes, in a stupor I watched the liquid filling the flask, it will help someone, you thought, and from this two hundred grammes drawn from me in five minutes, I worked out how long it would take to empty out the other five litres through a simple cut in the wrists.

'Good night, Josephine.'

I left that room, bled white.

I drew up at the kerb, got down to open the car door for Emilia: first came the plastered limb, then her whole person, the look in her eyes said she did not want to go yet.

'Are you going to see Doctor Y?'

I replied that the work was finished, so it was just as well to hand it over and be done with it.

'If I were you, I'd wait a few days first.'

She stared at the plain cover of the manuscript as it lay on the car-seat, there was something else she wanted to say and that I did not wish to have said to myself, and yet her silence blackmailed me, those slightly drawn features that she will have in the end, framed on the best mahogany.

'Emilia, you mustn't catch cold.'

I walked with her right up to the entrance of the Centre, asked what time I should pick her up at, a male colleague of hers arrived, we took a quick farewell, I got back into my car, drove along slowly in the traffic which is always dense at this hour, I could be sure Doctor Y had not reached his office yet, I had to take my time, and meanwhile think of a title for the book, suggest the pseudonym they should use, details I had put off till now.

The gaze that starts from the mirror may briefly linger, but has no answer to give. Likewise every thought of mine came to nothing before that sole question. I was being urged on several sides to pronounce on it, to do this speedily while there was time, and all the while my awareness of this obsession kept me in anguish, yet I could go on telling myself nothing new has happened, as if what mattered, after all, was no more than daily events, the streets, the houses, our encounters, our business dealings and provident cares, the goad of money which I have never been able to get away from, I could look the old grave-digger up again at the coal depot where he lived, it was not far from where I was driving that moment, I still had question to put to him, and in the meantime I passed by Porta Magenta, in a few minutes I would have reached San Siro where no one was waiting for me, in fact no one was waiting for me anywhere except Doctor Y, dear Doctor Y, I would tell him, I've some things I'd like to explain to you, my discovery that my characters were forestalling my (their creator's) intentions in what they did, wonderfully amenable to anything at all, to every sort of dark depths you work into them, that's it, I said, a lesson in absolute freedom, and soon after, waiting at the traffic lights' red, I felt ashamed at having said it, when a different truth showed against the light, the faint tracery of it rising above the design of what had been reality, and all that I had written, related, dressed up, in my stories to that moment, that cunning mixture of truth and mystification that is probably there at the origin of art, was no more than outward show: now that dominant thought lit up the scene, and what I had called experience had no value at all, it was a simple preliminary, without any of the significance I had attributed to it.

A howling siren compelled me to slow down, from behind me an ambulance went hurtling by, swerved and disappeared at the avenue's end. I was going to carry on to the race-course, then go back to Corso Europa, to Doctor Y's. Those messages taken altogether demanded a summing up, a gesture, and I was making a last effort to put off the business of accounting. Nothing has really happened, I could pretend to myself. Not even Miriam has ever existed. The fields, the open places around the habitations, stand white with hoar frost. The ambulance's passing had shaken me. I was trailing along close to the kerb, now the sight of the frost gave me strength again, I wanted to stop, breathe pure air, I passed before the shut gates of the race-course, turned right towards the stables and braked. Draped horses paced in the covered walk led along by grooms, I made for the jumping ring, the little box hedges shone in their powdering of frost, I had come here years earlier, I think, with Ric, to see some one he knew competing, I felt the sloping ground under my feet, gone hard with frost, and I was struck by the way that some unknown force continually drove me to the outskirts of the city, to sights that induced meditation in which the body itself had come to be absorbed completely now, happy to be stirring in that pungent air, the stable odour, the snorting of the quadrupeds, the political situation has me worried, Ric was saying, with the third obstacle already behind, I went back and sat beside him on the little stand, our binoculars followed the horsewoman to the wall, then to the water-jump, but at the triple fence the horse jibbed, I heard the voice over the loud-speaker giving the time and the number of faults, but none of it registered with me, Francesca was wearing a wide-brimmed hat, only Anselmi was missing to complete the picture, why don't you write a fine story for our next number? he made the offer without a trace of irony, I'd give you a pretty fee for it, we were leaning side by side on the wooden railing, he clapped a hand on my shoulder just as a red-roan cleared the five-barred gate to an outbreak of clapping, I hope you said yes, Ric murmured, Anselmi has taken a liking to you, the rider had taken off his hat to salute the judges, no one must know that you worked for Doctor Y, in fact you know what I am going to tell you?

The entry to the ring itself lay open, I put up the collar of my coat, things are over between us, Ric was going to say, over for ever, but I was describing, to Emilia, a disturbing dream I had had about Jo, Ric's tense profile slowly rolled from me on a fixed axis with all the others, I still looked out on blankness, anything you dream has its counterpart in reality, Emilia maintains, but the mechanism, needle point on graph, must have broken down if the unconscious can play these tricks, seeing Jo has never raised ideas of that kind in me, and nonetheless, in the dream, the voluptuousness felt in possessing her was great, Ambro encouraged me but in harsh tones, he had suddenly come back and he watched us tranquilly, I tried to give of my best, I enjoyed what I was being forced to do, in punishment, a recurring guilt complex, Emilia declared, and I was the only one who knew how far down the roots of it went and how imperative it was for me now to tell her, a painful estrangement for us both, I felt the compulsion to it throb like an artery: I laid my thumb on it and the thought of her relentlessly beat on: I must tell you about Miriam, you know, that girl.

At the cage horse and rider rolled over on the ground.

She came in without a word of greeting, threw the book down on the bed. From the gesture I understood at once.

'Just look and see how he's treated you.'

She sat down on the divan without taking off her

coat, I rose to turn down the music, asked her when she had bought it.

'This morning: it was on display in a book shop.'

I had forgotten all about it, though barely a week had passed since my night visit to Josephine. I picked up the book and looked for the part that concerned me, my name was listed in the index for a single entry, I found the page and read what was there, trying to hide my emotion from Emilia: Ambro had devoted nine lines to me, and that included the details of my publications.

'Unbelievable,' I murmured.

'But go on, take a look at the rest of it: there are people who're not worth half as much and he's written about them as if . . .'

For Ambro to have noted me down like that (leaving aside the question of strict critical judgement) was treachery pure in Emilia's eyes. Her weakness is that she always believes in other people and expects the best of them. As if what matters were what happens here and now.

'Well, what do you say to it?'

In spite of my disappointment I was tempted to find excuses for him. Although Emilia's indignation was more than justified, I could not share it, almost as if I had always expected as much, or perhaps this was the first positive result to come from that recurrent thought, the lesson it was to provide, the swine, Emilia was saying, it was the first hint of how we could face events, watching them explode around us, without being hit by them, or being afraid, they could walk right over you, she exclaimed, rounding on me now, and you would still find mitigating circumstances, I saw Ambro all over again, sunk down in his chair, that evening, in the house by the sea, his voice was saying: you make too many concessions, in your books, and today I knew that had not been a friendly warning but a final pronouncement, the sentence condemning me had already been phrased, set up in type, the conclusion was inescapable, by that time he must have written what we had only this moment read, it looked almost as if, in the act of handing down his last judgements to posterity, he regretted the enthusiasm with which he had greeted me in the beginning.

'At least you'll tell him where he can go!'

Emilia flattened her cigarette stub on the edge of the ash-tray, stretched out an arm to put off the record, but the Vivaldi concerto, cut off halfway through, continued in memory: I completed the musical phrase added it to the one before, in the pauses Emilia's words rang, because Ambro is vainer than a woman, she all but shouted, your sin is that you have never praised him up as so many others do, and, in fact, when it comes to him, my dear, a cruel happiness invaded me, the scene opened out, a wide landscape, the bow of the viola sawed through the trunks of ancient oak trees, I was stroking Ambro's skull as I sat by a spring, because the ones with less talent fall back on other ways and means, you don't have to raise your voice, I answered, unruffled, I was sorry for her sake and, above all, for Ric's, the miserable spite that lashes us through our days does not outlast death, it is true, but it constantly taunts Her in challenge, imagines it provokes Her, makes Her bat an eyelid, and a smile came over my features, it's great that you can laugh about it, was Emilia's comment, and we were worrying about the success of his marriage! but I was thinking of the risk I had run because, in those very days, I had thought of letting Ambro read the manuscript for Doctor Y.

'And anyway, think of it: if I had gone off with him, he would probably have written something quite different. Because you don't know what he said to me.'

'When?'

It had happened that morning on the shore when she was going out to the rock with Ambro, and Jo and I were following along behind.

'It's strange, he said to me, but I've a terrible desire to make love to you.'

There was a silence: I felt an eyelid quivering, a keen and rapid beat.

'Why didn't you tell me?'

She shrugged. She came over and sat beside me.

'I want you to go back to your writing, but in earnest. You've got to show him who you are, show all of them.'

I envied her certainty, her unshakeable faith in things, in the ultimate triumph of good, even that arm, bulked out with plaster, seemed a natural adjunct of hers, a band of firm and reinforced fibres, a strength I too had known and which now I was losing, being obsessed by a certainty which crushed all others, that allowed no more than fleeting defections in Emilia's arms. Or swift hallucinations, where Miriam was waiting impatiently.

'Where are you going?'

'Don't worry,' I answered, 'I'm just going out for a stroll.'

As the apprentices in overalls hang about at noon, leaning against the wall or squatting on the pavement, in the break from work: the light from the public clocks at early morning, its torch flicker upon the wet asphalt; a sky of stone, the crotched plane-trees lank as skeletons on the ring road, that leaden glow down on the horizon, the eyes of shop-windows, the factory-yard sky; the great statues 'after the Greek' standing on guard on the gallery staircases, the full-blown privates of rapt gods and goddesses, the crypt-like silence of the courtyards, that corpse-like marble, while the little iron lift steals upwards past balustrades, Corinthian columns, granite balconies, inaccessible attics: you've seen that it's nothing? she smiled, you mustn't be afraid.

Up high, perhaps scaffolding, the echoing blows of some one hammering, the noise of the traffic thinner now, the hammer takes up again blusteringly, I have never understood why this apocalyptic gloom calms me, the beloved winter of this city, I would like to have hugged her knees one last time, to have held her back, stopped her from going off like that, wait, I must explain to you, I had said to her, the two of us motionless by the pillars of the flyover for Turin, near the exit for Florence, leaning against the car, I was holding her hands on her hips, try and understand, I murmured, now that you have come back you must stay with your people, her belly thrust towards me, provoking, I tried to draw back, the cars whizzed by overhead, but I can't believe this, she challenged, her large eyes wide.

I had gone round our block but no more than fifty yards from it: if Emilia had come out on the balcony, she would have seen me standing before the wire-netting of the scrap yard, but I was much further away, I studied those twisted panels, the sockets of the headlamps, the bleak spectacle of those carcasses, the seat frames, the disembowelled springs on which Miriam used to give herself, at each new meeting that woman's haired mound on the child's body took my breath away, and each time something more collapsed in her, her headstrong no came less defiantly, her pupil rolled back and upwards, looking for a way out from this pleasure which seemed to lacerate her, then fallen back on the car-seat, two tears sprang to her eyes from happiness, the unnameable name, she would call it just that: happiness, because I love you, and now before those piled wrecks, those rusting bodies, I asked her pardon, I explained one more time why we should not see one another again, for your own good, Miriam, try and understand, but I can't bear it, she begged, it doesn't matter if you don't love me, I was never to forget her voice, her sullen look, so hostile to my silence which was condemning her to a return beyond the flyover, to the building where she lived with her people, I knew I would harm you, I had told her, the unceasing rumble of the cars made the pillars quiver, let's go away, us too, she said aloud, not believing in her own words, perhaps she was thinking of herself alone, but I was to understand that a little later, I had come into a life which did not belong to me, I had set it in a turmoil, and now I was saying to her, I have made a mistake, the story is over.

From under that mass of wreckage Miriam's voice rose invincibly. How could Ambro matter to me, his pettiness, my lesser or greater glory as a writer, when the true man in me was still given over to that voice? — if those metal plates were turning into granite, into slabs of compact black marble and shining monoliths which crush us, condemning us to our pits?

I took a step, meaning to go away: a bit of glass left in a headlight blazed out, I must do something, I thought, I swayed, inside me there was only emptiness, I felt devoured by the light, torn apart by the violence of these memories. So much wrong, I thought, so much wrong for nothing, how much useless suffering and all because I wanted those arms, that groin, the waxen breasts, the hair rising at the nape of the neck, come quickly, she breathed, her spread palm against mine, even her nails have grown again, don't be long, I'm waiting for you, and the ray of light suddenly went out, where Miriam had been, the gloom flooded, I still had the odour of her skin under my nails, and I, swallowed up with her in nothingness.

'But where did you run off to?'

'Just round about here. I wanted a breath of fresh air.'

Emilia looked at me gravely.

'There's been a call from your brother. Your mother's ill.'

She had already begun her meal. She did not ask me to join her. I picked up the car keys and made for the door.

'Wait a minute, I'm coming too.'

But it would have done no good for my mother to have seen her just then, with her injured arm: not only that: a sense of foreboding made me rush. At the old gateway into the street I ran into my brother who was leaving, he informed that the doctor had just gone away, he had put her on a drip, and she was resting now.

'But how did she manage to let them know?'

'Signora Bernotti found her this morning stretched out on the floor . . .'

She must have fainted, no one knows why yet, in getting up from bed, all this last week she has been harassed by insomnia and palpitations, and now she must be looked after, as the doctor said there was no time to lose.

I rang the bell of her flat, Signora Bernotti opened the door, said a good morning which sounded like a reproach.

'Come along, she's sleeping.'

I had to beg her to leave me alone, to go and have her lunch, I shall wait until you come back, you will certainly have to call in a nurse, she knew one who was so efficient, four thousand lire a day, she had already been 'on our stair', when Musazzi, that fine, upstanding man, suffered his death pangs.

'Don't you worry,' I said, 'I'll see to it.'

A feeble glow from the window giving on to the courtyard illuminates the room, the great bed where she looks smaller than ever, I came in troubled by a shadow, by resentment at myself for letting my private torment grow until I could forget hers which was so much more real, as I was sharply reminded now by the fumes from the spirit which the doctor had rubbed on her veins, she keeps her arm by her side, in a repose that has its grace, her fingers lie open, in acceptance, two strips of plaster hold the needle steady, from the inverted flask a yellowish liquid drains imperceptibly, and the hand itself looks false, no longer hers, her true one which she has never wanted to take off now

158

slips obliquely from her ring finger, hangs over the bony joints like a useless charm.

'Mum,' I whispered, and I felt myself flushing, with pleasure and shame, as I called her.

Her breathing came a little hoarsely, like a child's, her skin, the surface of her neck, heavy and thick as the pelt of late-autumn grapes, and, in amazement, I studied that mask which, for too long now, I had ignored, looking down on her, the iron stand beside me, lightly smoothing the sheets around her face, well aware that I was helpless before any eventuality at all, and my eye searched the room for the signs that always accompany Her destroying presence, but I did not come across one of them there, not a single indication, I watched my mother as she slept and I was already beginning to take leave of her, the waxed tiles shone as ever, the objects which partook of her immobility now, I walked across the room.

On the chest of drawers, a coloured photograph had been slipped into the wood edge of the mirror, the last one of her which my brother had taken the previous summer, her gaze is remote, with the look we notice in the deceased, everything from her has been analysed already: urine, blood, excrement and spittle, even her smile now appeared to be set in glass, item from a case-history, and what struck me in the illness was how like secret betrayal it is, I shuddered, this was the night before execution and no way out, but still, this time, I hoped in the shakiness of the accusation, or that she would not listen, distracted as she is by the infinite number of summonses that invite her to present herself.

'How do you feel?'

A crack between the eyelids, immediately sealed

again. My anguish is that she may go off before I can put this bundle of affection and resentment into words for her, can overcome the shame of talking and making gestures, really it is she who is my city and all that I bear inside me, in its name, the belt to her dressing gown is railings, her hand is full of courtyards, full of the steady battering of chisels, of worn door-steps, electric fires, street vendor's cries, malignant griefs.

I was in front of the chest of drawers, my fingers on the handles of the first drawer, I tried it and the draw moved out at the first jerk. It seemed unbelievable to me, there and then, that she should really keep a bank book, perhaps the only one in her life, with sums of money entered which she would give back to us, her sons, finally, without having had any enjoyment from them, but I knew, too, that what she feared above all in her own end was the expense this would have given us, and perhaps this is what she must have been thinking of, month after month, when she put aside the little I handed over to her.

I pushed the drawer in smartly, like a thief caught in the act. She had turned her head on the pillow and perhaps observed me from under her eyelids, as she would watch my father undressing, when he had just come home from another woman's arms.

She opened her eyes as the sound of a siren travelled up the street.

'How are you?' I smiled.

The way her eyes protruded from the sockets was startling, she stared at me, terror-stricken, the siren howled nearer.

'It's not coming here, you can sleep in peace.'

She shut her eyes again, I stole off on tiptoe, once seated in the kitchen, I lit a cigarette, and turned a kindly eye on what had been her keepsakes: the Singer in its corner, the oven-cloths she had decorated with stitch-work, the tin box for used matches, the table's marble top itself, but that, shining clear, now that all the cups had been removed, suggested with its cold surface how she might be laid out, that skilful way they have of peeling to the skull with knife and fork, the angry hiss of the trepan, please call me the chef, the skin of the head brought right over on the teeth, reversed, like a carnival mask, the quick, sure movements of the hands gloved to the elbow, because we have to accustom ourselves to this too, to the humiliation of a violent end or one that is, medically speaking, ambiguous, and I wanted to let her know what Miriam had suggested to me a short time before: that you are not to be afraid, and if anything the journey is short from the spot where we fall to the tree-lined square, to the gates by the building that is painted yellow, to the rose-bordered walk where the hearse stops, everything should be done in an under-tone, noiselessly, there is something so wrong in shouting close to the dead, and instead there is the slamming of the doors, the habitually excited voices, let the blind down a little, and the thud of the body as it is deposited on the recipient, the metallic starts of the trolley as it is pushed into the goods lift, the journey will not be long while the last blood begins to coagulate on the stainless steel, a chill trickle that soaks the hair on the neck, a narrow corridor, then it is introduced into the cell, past doors like those on a dairy's cold-storage room that are constantly opening and shutting, but here it is human forms that come and go, others that wait on the trollies, offering an image, moreover, already seen elsewhere, of a body

rigid on four wheels, too like the images from Ravens-
bruck, from Belsen, the sterilized infernos, of the
hanging loops, the round grips that sprout from the
ceilings, of the death-toll helpers in white overalls.

I went up to the bed and at once drew back: I did
not want to look at the shattered line of the jaw, the
pale little pouches of flesh under the chin which I
had already seen in a childhood photo of her (a
strange cross, of first constitution with last, to be
generated on this pillow), then it is true that we come
full cycle; and to think how tender our flesh is hurt
me — the story it is printed with, its stubborn resistance
to decay.

From the bedroom at times came her faint moan,
in the silence of the other rooms that near-sigh was
magnified, became unbearable.

I went back to her side and watched: her immobility
seemed to call for a gesture, I asked myself what,
was there anything I could do apart from accustoming
myself to her absence? I knew of one gesture alone
which would cost me something, the only one through
which I would be paying personally: to destroy the
manuscript which, for days now, I could not bring
myself to hand over to Doctor Y. All the questions
which, in these past months, I had imagined I had
found answers for, came back before me now, un-
resolved; if anything, fresh ones urged themselves,
and more strongly. I had gone all round the building
without finding a way in, my mother had not even
tried; perhaps she knew that it does not exist, and in
consequence she struggled, engaging her scant forces,
in hopes of pushing back the stages that awaited her:
time in hospital, last pangs, the funeral, and with
her eyes closed now she was asking me to pardon

her cowardice, I am trying to last out, she was saying to me, in the course of all these years I've grown fond of the thing I am, a thing of no account I readily admit, and I had always thought I would come to visit her one day and find the door on to the street half-closed as they made ready to put up the black of mourning; I thought of Musazzi, the ex-ticket collector whom as a youth I would meet on the stairs with the gold braid on his cap, an impressive man of military bearing, cut off by some obscure illness as he lay in his bed two floors below the room where my mother now lies, and then I thought that this time my father would show up and set foot in this house, after a good twenty years and more, to see her wrapped in cellophane, like an orchid that is being dispatched.

She had opened her eyes, she murmured something.

'Is there anything you want?'

She moved her chin in a sign to indicate the table, on a china plate I saw an envelope: the letter, delivered a few days earlier, came from Rome, from the Ministry, and finally announced that, allowing the claim advanced earlier . . .

'At last,' I smiled, 'that pension is coming to you!'

I read her answer in the wrinkles of her forehead that smoothed themselves out for an instant, then immediately returned.

'Don't talk now, you mustn't strain yourself.'

From the flask the last of the liquid dripped down, I noticed the bubbles inside collapsing.

'Would you like me to close the shutters?'

That, too, would be like her: to depart without any great flourishes, from this setting of her plain tasks, her complaints, her little starts of pettiness, with the percolator at the sink still bearing its coffee stains, the newspaper folded back at the 'In Memoriam' notices, testifying her untiring check upon those who are still with us.

Hearing her whisper, I went up to the bed.

'Don't send me,' came the words, 'to hospital, I wouldn't like that.'

I tried to reassure her by saying it had been a simple collapse, blame it on smoking too much, the worst was past, she was not to get ideas. But I knew how useless it was, when she had closed her own mother's eyes on a bed in a hospital ward.

'Tomorrow there'll be a nurse here.'

Her lips gave out a sigh of relief.

Of this much I was certain: it never happens in moments like this. In fact she spoke again, with the ghost of a voice: 'Just when they're giving me the pension.'

Power, like wealth, has a reassuring smell. The materials that go to make it betray rather less of their impermanence. Ric's office has this smell: from the thick-leathered upholstery, fresh flowers, carpets, his own linen.

'Take your coat off.'

'Ric, I'm in trouble.'

I caught no look of surprise on his face, it was as if he expected it, and this did not hurt, seeing that I had decided to go straight to the point and not round about it as prudence counsels on these occasions. I had decided to gamble his friendship on one throw: I need a loan, I added, Ric was dealing with a pile of newly-typed letters which he quickly signed and turned over, one on top of the other, did they send you your royalty statement? he asked without lifting his eyes, I had to explain that something more was involved, I did not want a loan from him as my publisher, I wanted it from him privately.

'How much?' he asked as he went on signing.

'Five hundred thousand.'

'Right away?'

'As soon as you can.'

The buzz from his desk-bell was answered by his secretary's appearing, she took away the tray with the signed letters, I thought she looked apprehensive at the sight of Ric opening his cheque book out flat on the desk.

'That's not all: I don't know when I shall be able to pay it back to you.'

The pen did not halt for an instant as it filled in the details, Ric detached the cheque and held it out to me.

'Thanks, Ric, I don't know how . . .'

'Forget it.'

I was grateful to him for not asking me anything at all about it, I knew what pleasure I would have given him if I had confided, and I knew as well how wholeheartedly he would have approved my course of action, but I felt I could never have confessed my motive in this, never tell him by what ways, by what obscure associations, I had come to so absurd and irrevocable a decision, I who had never had regrets, when I hardly dared confess it to myself: fear, Ric, I would have had to say to him, fear of this gentle companion who will never leave me and now that I know it I cannot draw back, a hundred and fifty pages, understand? hours and hours of work just to draw out from a story that I had already told and had no desire to retell, a different field of vision, a style, in short, some new feature to justify it: and all for nothing.

'How's Emilia?'

To talk about this would be difficult; and once more the spasm came, the stab of pain in my left side, again my eyelid quivered, a trembling of insect wings that nothing would stop, you see Ric so many things happen in life and this time it is nothing sensational that has come to pass, I do not even know myself why I did it, but last night I tore up those hundred and fifty typescript pages, that is to say, two million lire, and I have no money, Ric, perhaps you will think that I have not played altogether fair, but Edo himself said that you need courage, and it was the one gesture I could make, and now I have to give Doctor Y his advance back . . .

'When are you coming up for a flight?'

He did not ask how I was getting on with my novel, or wait for me to mention it, and I would have been glad to satisfy him, to assure him that I had progressed with it, that his trust was well placed.

'It'll be spring soon: then, the winds are right,' he added.

And we shall stand alone, looking Her in the face: neither family nor friends nor admirers there. I shall be alone with no one to help, it is for this reason too that I did it, I hope it will give me strength when the moment comes to have performed this sweeping act of renunciation, now that the previsions are only pain, bewilderment, and I know we shall lie motionless, at last, our mouths full of earth, our arms around nothing.

'Have you seen Ambro's book?' I asked.

'The Professor didn't exactly let himself go,' he declared. 'But we shall prove him wrong soon, eh?'

He held out his hand, I kept it in mine long enough to say everything I could not put into words: that if we have nothing to be sorry about, it will be easy to resign ourselves to going, and an unexpected strength rose from my heart to lips, a certainty of better times.

'You've been a real friend, Ric.'

'I hope so,' he answered without smiling.

'A violent man in Newark.' A few lines in heavy black type, some photographs, and he makes a path for himself, Tony Imperiale, with his short arms and the carbine gripped in his sausage fingers, the wet stain from his arm-pits, the sweat-shirt swelling out over his chest, the crew-cut and that tattoo of Snoopy on his right forearm, comes forward and says, filthy nigger: his eyes have grown small as small, I could even count every hair on that arm in the close-up where it holds the carbine bought in Newark, and he says, let's clear them all out, these filthy hogs who dirty the name of our country – but, how you've grown, Tony, and what a strong boy! – with their filth of drugs and sex and communism, and behind him his wife and daughter and a whole little forest of shotguns with their barrels oiled and shining, hey, Tony, this guy here says that we've not to harm him, and they all guffaw, their striped T-shirts stuck to their skins with their sweat, Tony the justice-dealer they call him, the Councilman of Newark, New Jersey, dumpy and solid as a bicep, with a neck all fat, there is no one to equal him at raising canaries, first side-tooth left side, covered in steel, I was certain that I had seen him before, this Tony Imperiale, when he sniggers that we've got to give a lesson to these civil rights people, and then as he unleashes a kick at the Negro's head and a straw hat shoots on to the pavement, I was less than a yard from him and I stared at him in fascinated horror, great, Tony, give him another one, and his forearm becomes a club of flesh, I bet there is little enough that moves under his trousers, a thing as thin as a finger, perhaps all his assurance comes from that, wow, boys, what a slap, and his vitality is so overbearing that it chases away, it obliterates every notion we ever entertain of our fragility as humans: so, Tony, tear his ear off with your teeth, and from within the circle of faces comes a muffled whining, a howl, the dull thud of the blows, keep back, boys, 'cos we've only just begun, I too drew back, I hoped he would be quick about it, this Tony Imperiale, and the stubborn will of the Negro was harrowing, I saw how, in our cowardice, we will cling to an existence of punishment even, just to stay alive, Tony's sweat-shirt dashed with blood, and that black bastard still wails, at every blow he gives a groan, perhaps because our fear is that the end robs us of the best that is still to come, our conviction on this score keeps life for ever in credit, now two of them are holding him up on his feet so that Tony can hit him, be quick about it, I prayed, give him this reward, too easy, laughed Tony, hey, junior, look over here at the photographer, and the faces in that ring, the good boys of New Jersey, roared with laughter, they knocked against me, they pushed, I had to laugh with them every time they glanced my way, there's lots more, panted Tony, raising up a hand, there's enough for everyone, he wiped off the blood he had on his hand by rubbing it under his armpit, my cowardice was so extreme that it paralysed me, now it was me they were striking, in that soft armchair where I sat, and my only terror was that I might stand it for too long like the Negro, in my dreams of being tortured I always end by telling the secrets, but this time it happened almost at once, also because the Negro was lying against the kerb with his skull split open, and a streak of blood ran from my temple, I was the first in line, stretched out at the wax-works, the attendants uncovered me drawing the sheet away with their fingertips, a gallery of corpses draped reverently, papier-mâché masks revealed as battered and bloody, the clothes ripped to shreds, struck down and fixed for ever in that instant, the limbs stiff, the faces swollen, the journey here was really short, this time I was the one to make it, laid out in the room for recognition, you're in a bad way, Emilia said, you look ugly today, there was the whirring from the refrigerator, I was waiting for them to ship me along the underground corridors, then on to the sandstone table, my name written on a plaster and the plaster stuck to an ankle, this is not me, I wanted to shout, this is only the wrapping, I don't understand where he's gone, Emilia whispered, there is something missing in him, I don't understand, perhaps it is because of this that She proves so alien to us, when we should have the same relation with Her, understanding and tolerance, that we establish with our own sexual organs, a habit of weakness and indulgence, of intimate secrecy to which every concern which is not purely carnal is alien, now I knew, as one of the departed, that She makes no more sound than petals do as they close about the pistil.

'A violent man in Newark.' Everything was in order: I folded the paper again and put it back in its place, there was the silence that attends great decisions, even the telephone's ringing had a wadded sound, I rose from my chair, it was four o'clock, I had chosen to spare myself nothing, not even the embarrassment of that meeting, not even the explanations I could have given in a simple registered letter.

'Doctor Y will see you now,' the young lady announced.

Emilia broke clear from the doorway of the Centre, crossed the street opened the car door.

'How did it go?'

'Fine,' I said. 'Am I late?'

Her hand closed over mine which I had kept on the gear lever, to communicate the relief she felt and also her satisfaction at not being mistaken.

'I knew you'd do it. How did he take it?'

I started up: now there was one last weight that we had to get rid of: the plaster on Emilia's arm, and on the way I explained to her that the conversation had been of the briefest, of course Dr Y had not understood a thing, he looked at me as if I were mad: Emilia laughed: did you bring the slides? I'm all prepared, but there was something else, a weight that lurked in the depths, of quite another nature, I tried not to attribute too much importance to my gesture, to think of it as nothing praiseworthy, there is one thing that you do not know, Emilia, that I have to tell you, about Miriam and in driving once more along that road to the hospital, I could measure what had changed in me meanwhile, I say 'stupid' to this, Doctor Y insisted, if the book doesn't feature your name, where's this dishonour?

'And then he said to me that I'll regret it: that I lack courage . . .'

This accusation still rankled, even if I did not admit that Doctor Y fully understood—and I myself was perhaps ignorant of them in part—the motives in my refusal, which, itself, had come too late, perhaps, to make them credible, and moreover I had put them to him confusedly, in the few minutes that our meeting lasted.

'One day,' Emilia commented, 'you must tell all this to Ric. You'd be making him a gift.'

We had trouble finding parking space, the appointment was for four o'clock, but already a little crowd was serried there in the hospital basement.

'I'll come with you to see your mother tomorrow.'

I was struck by the way the association had sprung in Emilia at the sight of the out-patients room: of course, we should go back to her together, now that she had ridden out the crisis and perhaps any need to go to hospital too, we had to do something for her before passive acceptance crushed the hope of keeping her alive, before one of those epidemics that the old grave-digger told stories about assaulted the city, eighty a day reaching the municipal cemetery at Musocco, and there is not enough earth to go round.

'We're in time,' I said, 'they've just called seventy-one.'

The wait on the benches was unnerving, every so

often the door of the plaster room opened on the corridor and a wrestler in a white smock came out, called a number, disappeared. I had had a sleepless night, Emilia turned on her side, had laid her plaster shield beside me, and so I had gazed at it for a long time, looking for a sign, one that would reassure me about the decision I was on the point of taking, and through the plaster I divined Emilia's skeleton, the Biro just lifted stopped paralysed above the stretch of white page, the hand hesitated to strike the first typewriter key, how could I translate this anguish into finite words? Intelligence looked on powerless at the debacle. Years of study, of regular practice, of desperate, mad application came to nothing: I wondered if the broken bones had really knit, and the outlines of her bones became a hydrographical chart, a whole geography of ligaments, reliefs, weird figures, unknown flags, allegories, apocalypses in miniature, a nightmare which a huge pair of scissors would cut away.

'It's our turn,' Emilia's voice said, rousing me.

On the threshold we passed a young man coming out, hobbling on a metal crutch, Emilia stripped, they queried the slides, then the scissors started on their tearing path from the shoulder down, a slender limb emerged from the covering, so thin and pale it startled you, there was a smell like fresh bread in the plaster room, the still-warm elbow casts dropped in corners, Emilia gave a start the moment her arm was touched, from the X-ray section other wrestlers emerged with slides, pulling apparatus furnished the room, the floor covered by a thin coating of flour, eighty-four, they called again, eighty-four!

'Try and move it,' the doctor ordered Emilia.

A Beer heater unit would do the rest: we are at a service station, you thought, dead cells crumbling to powder like the finest flour while I helped Emilia to dress again, on the screened-off cot alongside I sensed that another repair job was beginning, I was in a hurry to get away, to leave behind this vision of so much fragility, it tormented me to be confronted by the resistance the body offers to the cruellest damage, considering the time when the last crash would come.

'We'll take up tennis again,' smiled Emilia as we escaped from the place.

She insisted that we eat out, it was an occasion for celebrating, but in her, too, there was the uneasiness born of a nameless malaise.

In a diary I would have made this entry: Wednesday, 12th of March, naked before the refrigerator's open door; bliss after making love, body's fulfilment, on the further side of which we get a clearer image of the end (so it is clear that only civilizations in full flower can reach this awareness).

But I have never kept a diary, and then Emilia, on the bed, was waiting for the rest of the story.

'Go on,' she said, taking the glass from my hand.

Now, at long last, I was coming to the hardest part: the few days Miriam spent in the room where I lived alone, when she had presented herself on the doorstep with a case full of her clothes, she had made up her mind to cut herself off from her family, so as to live with me, she told me, and I who had never enjoyed her at my ease, who wanted her at any price . . .

'I don't know if you can understand that.'

Emilia nodded, we were looking at the opposite wall, propped up, side by side, on our pillows, we had already talked of this: and so after two days I told Miriam what I had always known, that in the long run I would tire of her body, that perhaps we were not made to live together, and she should go straight back home before it was too late.

'This is something you've already told me,' Emilia broke in.

I had decided to give up my job, to see if I could live part by my books and part by writing for the papers and television, I did not want any other burdens. But not two weeks later I was the one to look her up, she was never in to take a call, so one evening I went to pick her up with my car as she came out from evening classes, I confessed that I could not work, that we had to see one another again, if only she had not listened to me, instead she wept from happiness, I am the woman in your life, that's it, isn't it? She was so different from the girl I had first touched, except for the thing which had bound me to her and which every time I came back to, with frenzied demands, but Emilia knew all about this, too, and now I had to be careful and not succumb to the temptation of infecting her with my memories, I had to keep my hand from straying towards her, because this was the last appeal I was making.

Emilia listened but asked no questions. I drank down the last of my beer and put out the light. I did not remember how long that second interlude with Miriam had lasted. Perhaps all summer; then I tired of her again, or perhaps there was an upsurge of good sense in me, one more goodbye to Miriam, who could not believe it, after she had observed herself clinging to me in the mirror adorning my room, she was sure that I would give in, but after a month she was the one to yield, she phoned to say she must talk to me, under the flyover near her house, and it was our last meeting. Miriam had just got up from sick-bed, her fever had left her thin, the eyes, sunk back, made her gaze remote, I can't go on like this, she murmured, I can't go on like this any longer, it's not my fault if I love you, I could hardly take her for the same girl, she aroused so little desire in me with this last offering of herself, and so I found it easy to repeat no, for her own good it was better to finish things.

'For her own good?' Emilia remarked.

We were coming to the heart of it. It must have been after midnight, from the street came the passing roar of a car, then a man's laugh from the floor below, perhaps one of Mary's clients, and I had still to explain how my self-love had condemned her.

'What then?'

The words would not come easily. I had never yet confided to anyone what I was about to tell. Miriam got down from the car, perhaps she knew what she was going to do, but I could not even dream what that was, only, a week later, I remember I was walking along, reading the paper . . .

I rose from where I sat, my heart was going like a hammer.

'She had thrown herself down from the balcony,' I managed to say.

Emilia started, uttering a half-articulated sound. I stared wide-eyed in the gloom and saw that little item again, a piece of local news set down with all the others, name and surname, the reasons for this tragic action are not known, the next day, crushed, and afraid, I left for the mountains, horrible days marked by the terrifying black gashes I saw on her face and body where she was laid out in the recognition chamber. But Emilia was not following my account of it any longer, she rose abruptly from the bed, groped in the darkness, the flame of the match lit the bitter droop of her mouth.

'But how could you?' she murmured more to herself than to me.

Riveted to my pillow I felt that only now had I killed her. Now that I had told her end, Miriam was truly dead for ever. How could you keep quiet about it, Emilia exclaimed aloud, for all these years? And I who go mad with trying to understand, she shouted, I shudder to think I have revived her with you here on this bed, lower your voice, I say to her, but we've hardly begun, she put the light on, she went over and sat down on the couch as if to show me the repulsion she feels, yet I am not trying to defend myself, I had wanted to tell her about this before, but my courage had always failed, and then her irony inhibited me every time that I hinted at this obsession of mine in general terms.

'Now I understand: it's not death that frightens you, it's your past.'

The prospect of arguing it out at heat revolted me, but I wanted to say that perhaps they are the same thing, and that was why I had destroyed the work done for Doctor Y, to come before Her without too much remorse. Or through one last act of cowardice?

'But did you love her, even for a moment?'

I could not say: a thirst to enjoy her that was much

dirtier than the money paid to a prostitute. There were no attenuating circumstances except the body she withheld, her all-deriding eighteen years of age, her pale face and her rounded flesh, any dress on her looked awry, made to be ripped off, it is perhaps because of this that I have kept her alive all these years, so that in pleasure she could live with us again, in the full power of the senses, at the peak of life.

'Miriam was nothing, she would never have been anything,' Emilia's voice cut like a blade, 'but your imagination magnified her until she became everything. It was you who killed her. You fill me with horror, understand.'

I rose up too. It must have been very late. The room looked like a stage set, the bed, a wreck, glasses scattered about. From Mary's flat came the sound of water running in the pipes. I had foreseen the setting but not the dialogue, or perhaps I had counted on Emilia's being merciful, less forbidding.

It is plain enough, she could say to me, where your obsession comes from: too easy, laddy, to live with phantoms.

I did not know how to answer her: I saw my mother lying back bloodless on the pillow, her felt slippers by the bed, music played by a brass band, a march, if I could at least convey this anguish to her, but, no, my voice betrayed no change, so in the end her fury will prevail over my silence, it's your coldness that drives me mad, Emilia cried out, towards four in the morning, I was aware I had wounded her, she has said to me too often, take me, I'm Miriam, too often has the ill in me beaten her science, and a couple of paces away there were those felt slippers that she had sewn together herself, proof of a venture that had been cut short, the unfinished masterpiece that the treasures of the departed suggest.

'It's late, Emilia, come to bed.'

She had not stirred from the couch, the ash-tray in front of her brimmed over, I rose and opened the french windows a little, the night breeze quaked in the curtains.

'Where this ferocity of yours springs from . . .' Emilia said, thinking aloud.

If anything, I was as dazed as she was. Suddenly the sickness rose in me again, the same sickness at myself that had come over me that morning as I read the news; once more, conscience having buried Miriam's image, the original question that had posed itself as I went down into the tunnel near the Shambles was opening right out on to the void. And what was happening in me showed so clearly that Emilia rose from the couch, came over beside me, took up the whisky bottle, turned to me with a glass.

'Drink this.'

I did not try to meet her gaze. Her challenge comes in different terms: it asks that the bond between us should hold against the wear of passing days, asks the certainty of being able to understand, a little at a time, every event, every deviation.

'I must go and see Edo,' I murmured, 'must get him to listen to me.'

I hoped to provoke her, shake her. For her to forget my story with Miriam and discuss what is in store for us. Instead she was silent, distracted by the loose ends of my confession, and all the time I envied her coldness, the capacity that never deserts her to classify and distinguish.

The torment comes from the notion that we shall

178

be divided, our inner unity shattered, and you no longer know where you will be, where the truly untouched part of you will beat, whether in the mud or in the fir-wood of the casket, in the earth or its micro-organisms, this matter that is composed and decomposed, diaphanous tongues and black of velvet, crystal bubbles disembowelled by geometrical sections, the perfection of the drop, with your heart, all but stopped, keeping time with its last beats, that dull throbbing that now passes into things, a universe in the gaseous state, then one with liquid forms on the first day of the creation, and while She approaches with step not human, we have never been so desperately attached to life, in the lucid, unending anguish of the living, now that we know that the death of the cells is no more than an episode.

'Look,' I said, 'day's breaking.'

I pulled on the blind-strap a little. You're wrong about it, Emilia added, you can keep Her beside you as a companion, as you would like to, only if, inside yourself, you have already given up life.

Our bodies threw no shadow, in the room the lamp still shed that stagey light. I had no answer for her. I trusted in nothing but the wisdom which the thought of Her had begun to let me have glimpses of, to liberate me from the exorcisms which the way we live forces on us.

'Where are you going?'

Yesterday's clothes lay scattered about. Hurriedly I put back on what I had worn then. A chink of light, the consolation in the unending change among the elements, an intuition that will never amount to certainty.

Sitting on the edge of the bed, her face clasped

between her hands, Emilia stared at the blank before her. For a moment I hoped she might rise and put her arms around me.

'How much do you need to go to Paris?'

'Forget about it, I'm already in debt to Ric.'

The lock clicked home loudly, I had never gone out at the hour, in the silence of dawn.

Emilia asked for nothing more. I was going to bury Miriam.

In the stones and little domes, in the bronze fictions, in the marble volutes, in these pyramids and curving roofs with their gates barred like banks, in these mausoleums their haughtiness has not been chastened: the torch, the capital, the acanthus leaf, the Babylonian tombs of great Lombard families, proud juggernauts in glass and diorite, festoons, chapels, arks and pinnacles smeared with pigeon droppings, stand across from one another along the walks, the statue's elbow lifted high, in the anguish of endless grief, but with something voluptuous in the gesture that only they appreciated, alpha and omega on the wrought iron, engraved above the name of the great escapers, monograms to be shown off like diamonds, Latin mottoes in Byzantine mosaic, in Candoglia marble, cell gratings, neo-classic cloisters raised up to heaven, the stony heaven of the duchy of Milan, and black clusters of bodies thrust into the void, weep, unsated soul, to outweigh vine-leaves in iron, sphinxes, plumed fans, obelisks that rival the conifers, even from the yellowed photographs in oval frames, faces gaze out that seem never to have known happiness or pleasure;

in their look there is only the regret of not belonging to our number any longer, while the agile arm of the Orenstein Koppel excavator dives into the earth and leaves that orange gash, like some unclean tapir, in the middle of the black for mourning and its rusty claw gropes stubbornly right to the roots of the nearest mausoleum, shaking the little spires of it, now you can hear a metallic knocking of the safes, carefully sealed, in these travertine forts, grim keeps that await your name, that were raised by our fathers to stand guard over ultimate nothingness, certainly Miriam did not rest here, perhaps I was deceiving myself yet again, or I lacked the courage to look for her among the endless plots of the Municipal Cemetery, among the fragments of clothing and rotten wood turned up by the spade, and it is this I shall have to learn: a body being robbed, still warm, of its organs, spleen, kidneys, heart, amputation of the corpse, unique features that will live again in other bodies, and our romantic myth about death, the rightly-derided cult of the mortal remains, centuries of custom and prejudice overturned by a scalpel which cuts and divides, it will not be easy to accept the idea that it can happen to us, too, this sundering of the flesh that cellophane, zinc, lead, strive to defend.

Sprawled on top of her, I saw again the broad plateau of her belly, hollows and plains, on a wide screen, in seventy-millimetre splendour, the ear picked up brief harmonies, the dripping of alembics underground, you were the death of me, came the sigh, fluids and lymph in a printed circuit, I drew away from her body to devote myself to her knees, a continent emerged from the flood, I was lost in its swirls, once more I rested my ear on her to catch that infinitesimal gurgling, until her decayed hand spread on my shoulder, soothed the muscles of my back, drew figures, scenes.

I was looking for a place now where I could bury all this: but the marble of charnel house, crypt, court room, marble as rite, prayers recited, punishment, those surfaces asking pardon, those corridors of pain leading into silence, would never have her. So Miriam was safe. And I did not ask her to forgive me, I felt no other guilt than that of having desired her too much. I walked on at random, alone, watched by determined angels. Where a man had been, with his genius, a darker mark has been left, a pool of acids run from the cracks.

What did you imagine? said Miriam.

And yet it comforted me to know that under my feet were the juices that nourish the clay that makes the green weed stronger in its assault upon the tombstone's edge, here where the ivy climbs with official authorization, almost always on the south side, looking towards the Simplon, because we are those exhalations, the crowding of intestinal gases, the last drop from the ambelic: below the few houses, between the lava and the clods that give wine, I have noticed them, behind a rise in the Umbrian countryside, laid out in files and covered over like well-planted vines, in a purity that was enviable, the moss invading the stone, calcified, the wooden crosses, names come from far countries to die at the foot of a cypress and they sink lower under the hooves of the white ox; shattered by projectiles, those shinbones ring as clean as bells, I remembered the old man's words now, that revelation of his that consoled: but what worms? it is the rain that washes everything away, you have no idea how it filters down and down, how it cleanses . . .

And then in the darkness there was, as it were, a great light, in that dark beneath the slabs, in the earth turned up for fifty years now to make space for burials, a blinding light, and the indivisible showed as divisible, and what was fixed appeared in motion, as if a fleeting miracle allowed me to see what, in the natural scheme, I had till then been kept from seeing, the secrets of the earth, atoms and molecules drawing life from our body, and they were all round me, mutely, like a huge, silent arena. No greatness, they said: nothing.

But the answer, Miriam?

Thunderstruck on the terraces, they gazed on at a show which had been interrupted. Like the course of an illness, Her presence had come at me in cycles, moving its attack nearer and nearer. Today I gave myself up, exhausted, at the last station: to know if death is the prize for having lived, or its punishment.

And the courage Edo urged me to have, what was it, its exact nature?

Go on looking, Emilia replied.

The man with the spade observes me distrustfully, he watched me till I turned the corner, I let myself be carried along in the wake of a van, in the gutters little beaches of snow resist, the track of the tyres stops at a rectangle of dug-up earth, nails, splinters of wood, clues from the latest slaughter, his life was a panting after good, and that stab of pain, intense though so short-lived, forced me to stop halfway along the alley, a prospective of yew-trees clipped to cone shapes, from the far end a hand-cart advances, and on the hand-cart there is only a black drape, a dowager in a fur coat followed that little that the earth gives back, the attendant pushed on obliquely towards the gallery with the burial niches and the plastic flowers and only when they were lost to sight under the arched ceiling, did I dare to take another step, vainly I looked for some meaning in that apparition, vainly I questioned, asked those portrait busts, those beseeching orphans, what sense there was in that crime just committed, this is why our cowardice wants them to be alive, this is why it copies their likeness in bronze, the uniform, the sabre, and gives a coat of varnish to the gate, cuts the grass of the little plot over them, the thought that Miriam was not of their number brought me relief, that she had escaped that pitiless latin, where a little cherub torn from his dear ones points to the north, it is so easy to believe that it is true, that we shall be united with our loves, that this gurgling from the fountain is only an interlude, this limestone crib had never struck me before as a thing so familiar, Kyrie elison in porphyry, fluttering of chaffinches: the sense of outrage spent itself, a barrow, the slab moved and no more, the last troubled breathing and the pattering of earth on wood, an echo that is immediately deadened, Miriam was trying to say something to me, her lips moved but made no sound: that we shall never be so alone as here where we are treated as one, stowed away side by side, here where the gesturing figures ask pity and the chisels strike with muffled ring, the grave-diggers rig traps in a shelter, wood-smoke, forks, spades upright on the sky, rakes for the last brush-down, then the mournful call of the thrush over everyone, I am ready, I said to Her, just let me talk to Edo.

From the lopped arms of the lime trees, my dead

hung down, incorrupt, their lips sealed, keeping their secret.

'My case'.

I had left it on the platform.

Emilia handed it up to me through the open window. I had never seen her struggle to keep back tears, on another occasion perhaps we would have joked about it.

'Just two days and I'll be back', I said.

'You haven't even bought a paper to read'.

The pointer on the big clock jerked nearer departure time. I leant out to take her hand.

'Edo and Denyse will be furious with me for not bringing you'.

'I'll be waiting for you', she said in farewell. She turned and went, as soon as the train's motion had broken our grasp, not looking back once.

The compartment was half empty. I went and sat by the window, but a moment later I was on my feet again in the corridor, watching the familiar skyline, all blocks of flats, filing by, you have to see this out by yourself, she said more than once, it's better that way. I had asked her to come with me, but I knew she would not agree. Her gesture had been so unexpected and swift that I had no alternative.

But why did you do it? Well, what use did it serve? Her only possession with real money value, a little solitaire diamond, sold in the course of the day, to pay my journey to Paris. And in a few minutes she had packed me a case while I kept trying to explain to her, and while I was trying to, the objections I could have made became ridiculous before they were even uttered.

Because there is no happiness except in giving, the train was picking up speed, perhaps this was what I had still to grasp, but have you ever asked yourself if I am happy? said Emilia's farewell glance, but good-byes have never been our strong point, I must tell that to Edo, too, it exhilarated me to think of the surprise I was going to give him, but look who's here, Denyse, he will call from the doorway, this time it would be different, I have come to find out, and if the only way of facing up to Her is to understand what happens to us, Edo must tell me everything, you know what Emilia says? old age frightens me, not death, and I was ready to store up carefully every confession of his, anguish, bewilderment, uncertainties, and how he had emerged from them.

The train was entering a long curve, I recognized the open spaces, the chimney stack of the Shambles, and, further over, the roofs of our district, just an hour previous, as we were leaving the house, we had run into Mary right at the door, she was in great form, dressed in the fashion, I'm leaving tomorrow myself, she had laughed, but I am not coming back, I've found a place in the centre of town, sharing with a girl friend, I tried to look objectively at those city out-skirts, with the airport right up against them, the clattering of bogey on rail was beginning to soothe me when we slowed down, just beyond the flyover, now we were gliding forward on the embankment, the factory for ashes is in Via Zama: the sham work-shop where white vans drive in by the dozen appeared in the window, the two incinerators, the shaggy mane of the thorn hedges around the municipal dog-pound, I shall tell Emilia, do you know we live where they destroy? this refinery of burnt remains, its huge chimneys, the naphtha furnaces, the chute-mouths embedded in the concrete, the train slowly skirted the Crematorium, it was strange that I had never consciously noted the fact, we live among the lepers, where everything is done away with, the itching dogs and the refuse, the slaughterhouse that burns the remains, perhaps even the pupils of this rickety school beside the gypsies' bivouacs, the mounds of bottles and waste-paper, Mary is right to go away from all this, you need courage to stay on here, beside the compounds that preserve the materials that escaped the massacre, and once more under a colourless sky, that no man's land, plastic shapes, rips of polythene, flotsam thrown up on the beach, so it was no chance happening that the first hint had come to me on the by-pass round the Market, the gypsies are camped, among rubbish, in shattered buses, the bushes themselves are like knives, a bonfire wavers near a ditch, skirts brushing that filth, then an attempt at something like gardens, the train slowed down on purpose to let me see, a despairing lock protected it, vegetable plots full of dirty snow, and an arm shook something out of a window, an action of mother's repeated every morning, for years on end, she was the one I was coming back to, no flowers on these balconies, the desperate voices of Southerners in the grip of our frost, how had the miracle of Miriam flowered among them?

I felt my stomach threatening sickness; on the other railway-line, petrol trucks filed by on their way to the firing-line. Now I knew: death lives here, at Signal Box Number Fifty, at last I had recognized Her, surrounded by Her testimonies, refuse and slag, on

this eve of what awaits us, here where the city's line-
aments are lost, high walls and barbed wire, channels
and ditches, She would set out from here to reach my
mother, powerless I saw Her coming out of Her lair,
a broom will sweep this place where our feet have
rested, it had done me no good to try and be familiar
with Her, to cultivate Her image, call on Her day and
night, I must warn Ambro, I thought, because it so
happens that our minds always raise themselves above
our character, and our constancy falls below our
talent, and our faint-heartedness is greater than all
these things, thoughts on human qualities shaken out
by the train's speed, and yet I went on hoping, went
on looking for some sign, it is the beauty of being
alive, Edo explained, ask no more.

Trees, girders, fields that others will till. I stood
alone in the corridor, I was racing along in a deserted
train, but no longer in fear, aware that I was not running away in any direction, then I got down at the
Gare de Lyon, I reached the square, I rang at the door,
the concierge came out of her quarters in response,
she looked at the case I was carrying, there's some
mistake, she said finally, they don't live here, a fault
had developed at some point remote from us, never
heard the name, she added; listen, I told her, that's
impossible, I came here a few months ago, I rang
this very bell . . .

You boasted of your happiness, at being alive in
this world, you said you wanted to share everything,
and at the end you were alone, with a case too heavy
by far, in the vast hall of a station, the glittering night
outside the window, the loudspeaker repeated the
invitation twice, you bore the ache in your arm, as
it held the case, with joy; a last whistle along the

platform, they will come to fetch me, I thought, now that I could give myself up to watching the play's end, my mother in the bed that is too big for her, Emilia's petrified grief, Miriam's certainty that I would come to her where she was, in one of the front carriages, the slamming of the doors which had a sense at last, like the wind that blows icily at this point on the platform. Because only death sheds light upon life.